CW00643883

SOLVE OR COMMIT?

The Crime is in Your Hands

SparkPool

Published in 2024
First published in the UK by SparkPool Publishing
An imprint of Igloo Books Ltd
Cottage Farm, NN6 0BJ, UK
Owned by Bonnier Books
Sveavägen 56, Stockholm, Sweden
www.igloobooks.com

0924 001
2 4 6 8 10 9 7 5 3 1
ISBN 978-1-83544-210-4

Written by Em Bruce
Additional puzzle compilation, typesetting and design by:
Clarity Media Ltd, http://www.clarity-media.co.uk

Designed by Simon Parker
Edited by Alexandra Chapman

Printed and manufactured in the UK

Contents

About this book 4

Instructions 6

Puzzles 8

Solutions 232

About this book

This interactive book puts you in the driving seat of your very own criminal cat-and-mouse chase – and you can choose whether to be the cat or the mouse!

There are two narratives running through this book, and three different ways to read it:

1 You can adopt the character of The Skeleton Key and flex your code-breaking, safe-cracking, lock-picking muscles as you try to audition for Vicehaven's most notorious criminal gang – all while staying one step ahead of pesky law enforcement.

2 You can take on the role of Detective Robin Marlowe and push your sleuthing skills to the limit as you follow your instincts, your sharp mind and the evidence to snap at the heels of the latest criminal scourge on the city.

3 You can follow the story chronologically, hopping between The Skeleton Key and Detective Marlowe's storylines as you help these two evenly matched foes fight it out across the city of Vicehaven.

Whichever way you choose to read it, the crime is in your hands...

The Skeleton Key

Meet The Skeleton Key – a young, cocky, have-a-go crook meandering down the wrong path in life. During their turbulent childhood, a stranger once showed them how to pick locks, and it was like a light bulb switched on in their mind. Since then, The Skeleton Key has been on their own, armed with nothing more than their increasingly sophisticated lock-picking skills and their anonymity. This sticky-fingered thief has spent years pilfering their way through Vicehaven and now dreams of becoming a career criminal by joining forces with the city's most notorious criminal gang, led by the feared boss, Facade. In an effort to show off their skills, The Skeleton Key decides to target Facade's enemies, and it's not long until their criminal activities start to get some attention, but not all of it is wanted...

DETECTIVE MARLOWE

Enter Robin Marlowe, a straight-laced, determined and no-nonsense detective who is less than impressed that their superior, Inspector Conway, keeps assigning them to petty crimes instead of allowing them to get stuck into the more high-profile cases. Marlowe is young and new to the job, but already has good instincts and a nose for a clue. They are committing to cleaning up Vicehaven and are desperate to be taken seriously. At first, Marlowe puzzles at the seemingly random manner in which The Skeleton Key picks their targets, but the pieces soon start to fall into place as Marlowe realises they're part of a much bigger criminal conspiracy. Marlowe now wants to impress their superiors by catching The Skeleton Key – just as much as The Skeleton Key wants to impress Facade.

Instructions

A – Z PUZZLE

Each letter of the alphabet from A – Z has been removed from the grid once, to leave 26 empty squares. You must work out which letter from A – Z fits in each of the blank squares and write it in, so as to fill the grid and solve the puzzle.

ARROW WORDS

Answer the clues in the grid in the direction of each arrow to complete the puzzle.

BRAIN CHAIN

Solving this puzzle is simply a case of mental arithmetic. Move down the chain one step at a time, working out the next number based on the calculation in each box to reach the final answer.

CODEBREAKER

Work out which letter of the alphabet is represented by each number from 1 – 26, and then place that in the grid every time that number occurs.

JIGSAW SUDOKU

Place the numbers 1 – 9 once in each row, column and bold-lined jigsaw region composed of nine cells.

LETTER SUDOKU
Place the listed letters once in each row, column and bold-lined jigsaw region composed of nine cells.

KAKURO
Fill the white squares so that the total in each across or down run of cells matches the total at the start of that run. You must use the numbers from 1 – 9 only and cannot repeat a number in a run.

KING'S JOURNEY
Deduce the journey of a chess king as it visits each square of the grid exactly once, starting at 1 and ending at 100. The king may move one square in any direction at a time, including diagonally.

KRISS KROSS
Each word must be placed in the grid once to solve the puzzle – you must work out where each word goes in order to complete the grid.

PATHFINDER
Moving from letter to adjacent letter, can you find a path that visits every square and spells out words associated with the given theme? Start on the shaded square.

The Skeleton Key

Darkness has well and truly fallen over Vicehaven – the shadows are where I work best, and tonight's moonless sky will provide the perfect cover for the first part of my plan. I've found out that one of Facade's rival gangs operates out of a local business. As soon as I work out its name, I've got my first target.

<u>16 6 30 1</u>   <u>16 8 18 31 20 21</u>   <u>18 6 21 13 17 29</u>

6	23	18	30	7	11	14	22
A	B	C	D	E	F	G	H

13	2	31	16	25	17	29	5
I	J	K	L	M	N	O	P

3	10	21	32	8	12	19	27
Q	R	S	T	U	V	W	X

1	24	4	28	20	9	26	15
Y	Z	.	,	'	?	!	-

Puzzle 1

A: ....

8

Now that I've got my target, I just need to figure out where it is. The business isn't listed online (no surprises there), but I'm pretty sure this sudoku will reveal the map coordinates for me.

The correct order runs from left to right.

			7		3	1		
	5			8	2			◯
						3	8	
	3			9	1		4	7
		7		◯		8		
4	2		3	7			1	
	8	5					◯	
◯			8	1			7	
		2	5		9			

Puzzle 2

A: ....

DETECTIVE MARLOWE

I pull open the doors into Vicehaven PD to start my night shift and I'm hit with the familiar sights, sounds – and smells – of an overworked police department. I head to the board to see what new case has been assigned to me. Inspector Conway has this infuriating habit of writing letters as numbers and vice versa. I'm going to need another coffee…

Detective	Case no.	Description
12,1,14,7,4,15,14	5,1,A,X,7	13,21,18,4,5,18
13,1,14,6,15,18,4	9,2,P,D,13	11,9,4,14,1,16
13,1,18,12,15,23,5	6,4,B,H,2	20,8,5,6,20
13,1,18,7,18,15,23	4,17,C,G,5	1,19,19,1,21,12,20
14,1,22,1,18,18,15	20,3,R,L,8	6,18,1,21,4

Puzzle 3

A: ....CASE NUMBER.............

A: ....CRIME.............

Of course, another tedious case. I open
the case file and, with a frustrated sigh,
I note that the old printer has splotched
ink all over the victim's phone number.

Complete the brain chain to fill in the
missing numbers in the phone number.
The correct order runs from left to right.

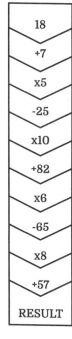

18
+7
x5
-25
x10
+82
x6
-65
x8
+57
RESULT

Puzzle 4

A: 9_7_-_2_-6_8

The Skeleton Key

I arrive at Lady Luck's and head to the alley to sneak in through the casino side door. I silently approach the door, and then stop myself. I've forgotten to put on my gloves! Phew – that was close. I'm hardly going to impress Facade by leaving my fingerprints everywhere. I reach into my backpack and pull out one glove, but where's the other one?

A **B** **C**

D **E** **F**

Puzzle 5

A: ....

With my gloves safely on, I flex my fingers in anticipation. I can see there's a combination lock on the casino side door. Picking locks is where I shine – my night is off to a great start...

 One number is correct and well placed

 Nothing is correct

One number is correct but wrongly placed

Two numbers are correct but wrongly placed

Puzzle 6

13

DETECTIVE MARLOWE

I call the phone number, but no one answers. I run the number and see that it's registered to a casino. There's a street number but no name, which is very strange indeed, but that's not going to stop a detective like me.

Unjumble the letters to find the aptly named street.

Puzzle 7

EFTSUOETRNRET

A: ....

Something about that address rings a bell, and with a jolt of excitement, I realise that's Queenie Royale's place. She's rumoured to be the head of one of Vicehaven's biggest criminal gangs. My night could be about to get very interesting... I go to grab the key for a patrol car, and there's only one left, the rest have all been claimed. Which key is it?

Puzzle 8

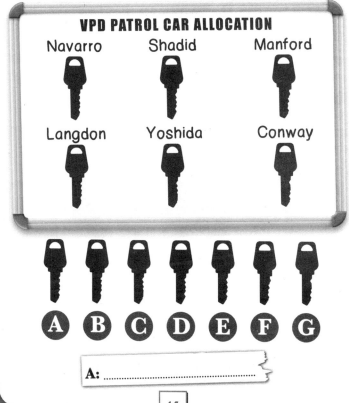

VPD PATROL CAR ALLOCATION

Navarro   Shadid   Manford

Langdon   Yoshida   Conway

A   B   C   D   E   F   G

A: ....

15

The Skeleton Key

I know that I'm here to leave a message for the criminal underworld of Vicehaven, but I can't resist the lure of the con as I make my way through the casino. After all, what better way to blend in than to play a few games, right?

I settle down at the roulette table and, using my sleight of hand, I distract the dealer and swap out the ball for my weighted one. I confidently place my bet on...

Puzzle 9

HGWICKTELEYTTANB

A: ....

I've cheated my way into a high-stakes game of blackjack with some of the city's wealthy elite. If I win this hand, I'll certainly put a noticeable dent in Lady Luck's takings tonight, which will make this job all the sweeter.

To win, I just need to play a club or a heart card higher than an eight. Luckily, I've been counting cards all night, and I'm pretty sure I know what's left on the table. Which card should I play to win?

A heart is to the left of a club.

There are two cards wearing crowns in the middle.

Nine diamonds sit to the right of a Queen.

The cards on the ends make a total of 16.

A king sits to the right of a heart.

A: ....

DETECTIVE MARLOWE

When I arrive, Queenie Royale is fuming about some have-a-go hustler who cheated their way to the casino's biggest ever payout tonight. I ask to see the report for all the chips cashed in today. How much did the cheat get away with?

Puzzle 11

Wednesday 16th October
Report: Chips cashed in
Time: 08:00–22:30

	Customer 1	Customer 2	Customer 3
Green	29	20	16
Red	8	3	2
White	43	34	49
Black	14	11	8
Pink	35	46	52
Blue	6	7	4

Black chips = £500 Blue chips = £100 Green chips = £25
Red chips = £250 White chips = £50 Pink chips = £10

A: ....

I can see that something has been torn off the bottom of the report. Could Queenie Royale be trying to hide something from me? I find some scraps of paper in the bin, but which one is from the bottom of today's report?

Puzzle 12

A
SECURITY NOTES:
10:32pm Suspicious vehicle spotted in the alley

B
SECURITY NOTES:
11:04pm Exterior electrical outage detected

C
SECURITY NOTES:
10:53pm Private office safe opened

A: ....

The Skeleton Key

Once I've cashed in my chips, I slip away from the casino floor, pull my gloves back on and head to the boss' office to do what I actually came for. Straight away, I spot the surveillance camera blinking in the corridor. I'll need to disable that before I make my next move. I locate the fuse box and carefully snip wire...

Puzzle 13

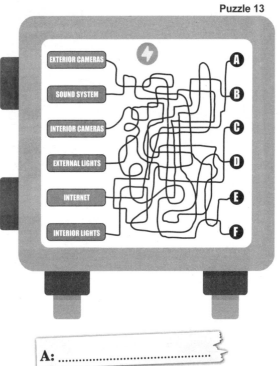

A: ....

With the surveillance camera successfully disabled,
I slip inside the owner's office and quickly locate the safe.
When I see it, I allow myself a small chuckle. As if this
measly keypad could keep out The Skeleton Key!

I know this is a four-digit code and that each number can
only be used once. I'm pretty sure my brilliant mind can do
the rest...

• The fourth number is a
  factor of the second.

• The sum of the first
  and third numbers is
  double the fourth.

• The third number is
  half of the first.

Puzzle 14

A: ....

DETECTIVE MARLOWE

Much to Queenie Royale's annoyance, I make my way to her private office. I can see immediately that someone has made light work of the top-of-the-range safe. I'm surprised to see the safe is still full of cash – it seems as though the thief was looking for something specific. A taunting note has been left behind; does this reveal what they took?

Puzzle 15

Under pressure is the only way I work,

and by myself is the only way I'm hurt.

I'm a type of red card,

but I am not a heart.

Of a promise

I am usually part.

TSK

A: ....

It seems like this mystery TSK made off with quite the haul indeed. Begrudgingly, Queenie Royale admits that the thief took something else from her safe, and this time, it's definitely personal...

Delete one letter from each pair to unravel the answer. For example, the code DB AO GL could be unravelled as D~~B~~ ~~A~~O G~~L~~ to make DOG.

FQ UO EC EP DN IL TE

GR OI YB AH SL EN 'ST

JL EU WC KB SY

MG OA CL WD ED SN

DC IO CG SE

The Skeleton Key

I've got a real spring in my step today. No one steals from Lady Luck's and gets away with it – but I pulled it off without a hitch. I'm sure it won't be long before word of my triumph reaches Facade, but I'm not taking any chances. I'm going to hit another rival gang tonight. It seems only right to let my souvenirs from last night pick the target, so I give them a roll.

Puzzle 17

Multiply the numbers on the dice to choose the next gang to target:

If it's a multiple of 12: The High Rollers
If it's not a multiple of 5: The Axel Grinders
If it's not a multiple of 6: The Brokers
If it's a multiple of 18: The Clean-up Crew

A: ....

The dice have spoken. I rack my brains to try and remember the name of this particular gang leader. It's slowly coming back to me, but I think this A – Z puzzle will fill in the gaps.

Puzzle 18

A		T			L			B			U	E
	A			N		S		U	A	T		
E		I	D	E	N	T		L		A		
	I		N		O				N			O
	N	E	A	D	I	N	G					R
	E			I		E		A		A		E
A	S	C		N	T		C	R	I	S	I	S
B		O			K							
				E	N	V	E	L				E
S	U	S			E		N			A		
M		L		B		L	A		T	I	C	E
A		I	N	E	R	T		L			T	
	A	P					B	Y	P	A	S	S

A B C D E F G H I J K L M N O P Q R S T U V W X Y Z

A: _U_ _E_ B_TL_R

DETECTIVE MARLOWE

By the next day, I still can't stop thinking about the robbery at Queenie Royale's. Inspector Conway dismissed it as no more than an opportunistic thief and told me to file it as 'unsolved', but something tells me this is no amateur. I try to distract myself by doing a puzzle in the Vicehaven Herald, but even this seems to be sending me messages...

Puzzle 19

RPR

IN

NGE

TS

FI

A: ....

Of course! I've been so focused on what the thief took that I hadn't considered what they might have left behind. I head to the evidence room, retrieve the casino chips that the mystery TSK cashed and dust them for fingerprints. Are there any fingerprints unaccounted for that might belong to our thief?

Queenie Royale
OWNER

Delia Swift
DEALER

Bill Banks
CASHIER

Puzzle 20

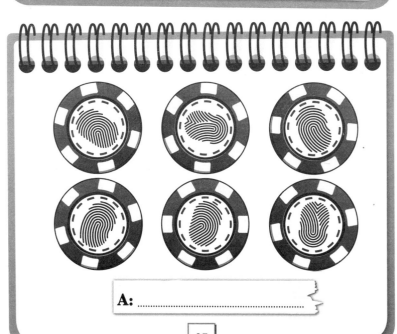

A: ....

27

The Skeleton Key

I arrive at the motel headquarters of The Clean-up Crew and assess the building. I know for a fact that Buster Butler's formidable private muscle has a room facing the street. If he's in the building, his light will be on and he'll be keeping an eye out for trouble. Is he in?

1. He has neighbours either side.
2. One of his neighbours is not in.
3. One of his diagonal neighbours is in.
4. His upstairs neighbour is not in.

A: ....

With that in mind, I move carefully across the street and towards the motel's back door. As soon as I step inside, I realise I've triggered the silent alarm. I've only got 30 seconds to enter the passcode or the alarm won't be silent for long...

The passcode is the word that doesn't appear in the wordsearch below.

Puzzle 22

N	C	C	T	R	V	M	P	E	X	V	W	O	N
B	O	G	R	I	F	T	E	R	M	O	B	T	M
J	N	H	R	R	H	E	U	E	U	P	E	L	B
S	N	W	Q	I	A	I	S	D	S	R	Z	Q	K
X	C	U	H	D	M	U	D	O	C	I	X	E	T
O	O	V	T	Q	O	Y	R	E	L	V	D	U	A
A	N	N	L	H	O	Q	S	I	E	A	I	R	R
Y	C	I	E	P	G	A	N	G	S	T	E	R	Z
D	E	F	T	W	F	D	P	H	G	E	I	V	Q
D	A	X	P	Y	S	K	B	K	C	P	A	Q	N
S	L	L	C	U	O	M	Q	L	P	P	O	U	L
C	X	K	A	N	N	M	U	R	S	V	L	S	S
J	Z	G	X	R	X	M	K	D	D	I	D	J	A
V	P	X	F	A	M	O	C	E	W	U	A	N	W

Gangster	Hide	Muscle	Grifter
Mob	Grimy	Safehouse	Alarm
Secret	Private	Squalid	Conceal

A: ....

DETECTIVE MARLOWE

Hmm... no fingerprints left at the scene. Just as I'm about to put the case file away, a warning pops up on my system. A silent alarm has been triggered at the residence of a high-profile target. I check the alert, but my clunky old computer has garbled up the text! Where is the alarm going off?

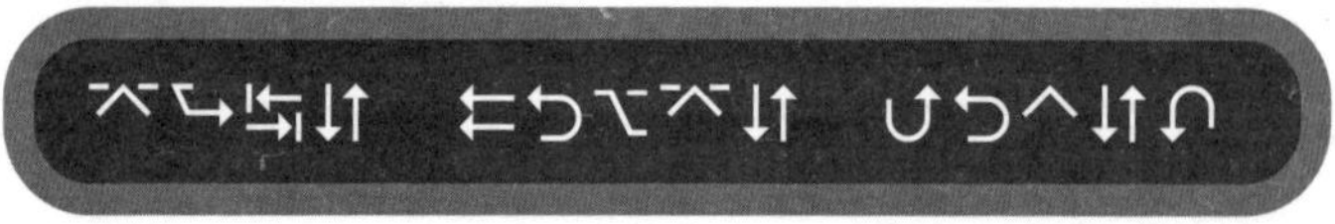

↳	⤶	↳	⇆	⇅	⇆	⇅	⬸
A	B	C	D	E	F	G	H

⇉	⇈	⇊	↶	⤻	↷	⤺	↻
I	J	K	L	M	N	O	P

↺	⟲	⌅	^	⌥	␣	⌣	⇪
Q	R	S	T	U	V	W	X

⇪	⇦
Y	Z

Puzzle 23

A: ....

Suddenly, the alarm deactivates. Someone must have entered the password, but I can't shake the feeling this is somehow connected to what happened at Queenie Royale's. I decide to check it out. There are a few ways to get to the motel, but which one will get me there quickest?

Puzzle 24

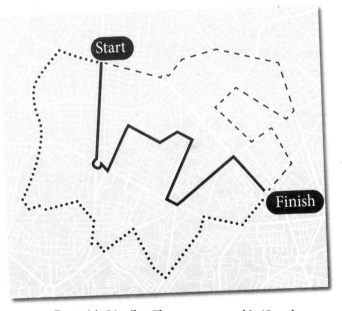

——— Route A is 34 miles. The average speed is 40 mph.
•••••••• Route B is 44 miles. The average speed is 33 mph.
– – – Route C is 38 miles. The average speed is 30 mph.

A: ....

The Skeleton Key

The password is accepted, and I tiptoe to the reception desk. I swipe a copy of Buster Butler's room key, but I can't exactly go bursting in if he's tucked up in bed. I need to pick a moment when I know for sure he won't be in. Luckily, my eye catches a note scribbled in shorthand next to the phone. If I can decode it, maybe I can pin down Butler's movements tonight. What does it say?

Puzzle 25

⼁	ᄂ	⼕	⼄	∟	⼙	⼓	⎮
A	B	C	D	E	F	G	H

⌵	⌡	⌅	⼁	⌒	⼂	⍺	⼁
I	J	K	L	M	N	O	P

⼁	⼁	⼁	⌐	⼁	⌵	⌣	✕
Q	R	S	T	U	V	W	X

⼁	⌇
Y	Z

A: ....

....

....

It looks like luck is on my side. I checked my watch when I disabled the lock, and it said 21:53. That was exactly 27 minutes ago. However, I also know that my watch is running 18 minutes slow (maybe I should buy a new one with my casino winnings).

Puzzle 26

Based on this scribbled note, how long do I need to wait before the coast is clear?

A: ....

DETECTIVE MARLOWE

I soon arrive at the motel. Just as I'm about to head inside, I spot something on the ground. Unjumble the circled letters to find out what it is.

4 letters
Aids
Case
Cash
Earl
Lust
Onus
Sari
Soda
Tore
Trap

5 letters
Alibi
Cedar
Cycle
Forum
Joist
Sushi

6 letters
Atomic
Eatery
Hearth
Yachts

7 letters
Enthuse
Hobnail
Results
Tabular
Unusual

8 letters
Alarmist
Twinkled

9 letters
Forgotten
Hierarchy

12 letters
Adjudicators
Authenticity
Cosmopolitan
Exhilaration

A: ....

I'm suddenly very aware that I'm alone with no backup, so I decide to call in my location just in case. It's not long before I receive a reply from Frank in dispatch, who only communicates in Morse code. I'm a little bit rusty – what does his reply say?

--/./.../.../.-/--./.   .-./././-.-./././..././...-/./-..
-.../.-/-.-./-.-./..-/.--./.   ---/-.
.../-/.-/-./-../-.../-.--

A: -   J: .---   S: ...   1: .----
B: -...   K: -.-   T: -   2: ..---
C: -.-.   L: .-..   U: ..-   3: ...--
D: -..   M: --   V: ...-   4: ....-
E: .   N: -.   W: .--   5: .....
F: ..-.   O: ---   X: -..-   6: -....
G: --.   P: .--.   Y: -.--   7: --...
H: ....   Q: --.-   Z: --..   8: ---..
I: ..   R: .-.   0: -----   9: ----.

A: ....

35

The Skeleton Key

Did I just hear a knock on the front door or is my imagination playing tricks on me? Either way, I should get in and out as quickly as possible. Now that the coast is clear, I slink up to Buster Butler's room and I'm greeted by another alarm. I know Buster always chooses capital cities as his passwords. I think carefully, then enter the numbers 237546. Which capital city is it?

Puzzle 29

A: ....

I slip into the room and spot the prize I'm here for right away. It's almost too easy! With a few moments to spare, I decide it's time to properly introduce myself to the criminal contingent of Vicehaven. I scan the room, then spot something that should put the word out nicely.

Unjumble the letters and add the missing vowels to find out what it is.

WPNRSP

Puzzle 30

A: ....

DETECTIVE MARLOWE

As I move through the silent motel, I hear a soft thud in a room above me. I go to investigate and find the door open. Something – call it my detective's intuition – tells me that something has been disturbed in here. Based on these two photos, what's missing from this room?

Puzzle 31

A: ....

This is all feeling very familiar. Could this be the same audacious thief that hit Queenie Royale's casino? As I'm about to leave, I spot a strangely marked-up news article that might answer that very question.

Vicehaven Herald

THIEVES PAINT THE VPD RED WITH EMBARRASSMENT AFTER HEIST

Ron Waffle

In a shocking turn of events, Vicehaven Gallery was last night hit by thieves who made off with the gallery's pride and joy, the priceless Van Grift watercolour.

The stolen masterpiece vanished without a trace, leaving those in the art community heartbroken and demanding answers. VPD detectives looking into the incident have yet to identify any suspects, plunging the case – and faith in the VPD – into question.

However, a source close to the investigation, who asked to remain anonymous, has shed light on a possible lead. According to the insider, there are whispers circulating among the underworld that the notorious criminal gang, The Clean-up Crew, may be behind the audacious heist.

As the investigation unfolds, the fate of the priceless piece remains unknown, leaving both law enforcement and the community on edge. Will the authorities be able to apprehend the culprits and recover the stolen Van Grift, or will it remain forever lost to the shadows? Watch this space.

Puzzle 32

A: ....

39

The Skeleton Key

I'm sure there was someone on my tail last night, so I'm feeling decidedly jumpy this morning. I decide to bring up my timeline and hit two rival gangs' headquarters today. Which one should I start with?

Starting in the top left, join the hexagons by creating a new word that's only one letter different from the last. Each hexagon must connect to exactly two adjacent hexagons. The words in the grey hexagons complete the name of the gang's headquarters.

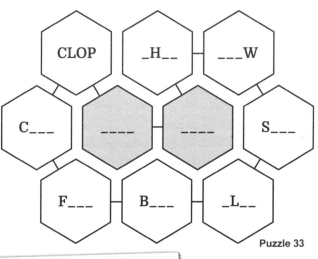

CLOP   _H__   ___W

C___   ____   ____   S___

F___   B___   _L__

Puzzle 33

A: The _ _ _ _ _ _ _ _ _

Yes, this is definitely the best option, plus it's not too far from my place, so I can walk there. It is a beautiful day, after all.

Plot the journey through Vicehaven by visiting each square once, starting at 1 and ending at 100. Remember, you can move horizontally, vertically or diagonally.

Puzzle 34

		48	47						26
51			91		38			28	
53	100	98							
		99		89				33	
		96			75				
		86				72		42	
	57	83			77	70			20
			79			68	66		
	5			60		62		18	
1				11	12		14		16

DETECTIVE MARLOWE

I'm itching to check the Organised Crime database back at the VPD, but I don't have the login details... yet. Unjumble the circled letters to find the password.

Puzzle 35

21	14	3	8		10	24	19	14	1	17	16	7
16		24		4		17		26		5		15
21	11	8	13	16	8	5		26	14	10	12	8
16		15		5		18		5		25		18
1	16	15	2	10	15	14	2	8	5	14	15	
26				7		23		9		1		7
8	1	26	17	6	23		1	10	15	10	8	16
5		5		10		13		14				24
	6	10	7	21	17	16	5	2	8	17	16	7
7		25		2		14		10		22		11
3	11	14	3	10		9	14	24	10	15	15	14
10		24		17		8		25		10		6
20	8	6	14	24	2	5	23		14	20	7	8

A B C D E F G H I J K L M N O P Q R S T U V W X Y Z

1	2	3	4	5	6	7	8	9	10	11	12	13
M	T						E					

14	15	16	17	18	19	20	21	22	23	24	25	26

A: ....

Hmm, no hits for The Skeleton Key in the Organised Crime database. Undeterred, I move onto my next clue – the photo of the muddy footprint. I know that the image is at 75 per cent scale, so using my keen sleuthing skills, I can work out the thief's shoe size.

Length (cm)	Size
23.9–24.5	5
24.6–25.2	6
25.3–25.9	7

Length (cm)	Size
30–30.6	8
30.7–31.3	9
31.4–40	10

Puzzle 36

A: ....

Muddy footprint = 22.5 cm

The Skeleton Key

I arrive at The Chop Shop to find an impressive-looking combination lock on the garage door. Hardly surprising, considering it's the headquarters of one of Vicehaven's most violent criminal gangs. It's just as well I love a challenge. What numbers should I turn the four question marks to?

Puzzle 37

A: ....

The lock gives way with a gentle pop and I slink inside. The one mechanic on duty is on a break, so I'd better act quickly. I'm looking for the beloved classic car of the gang leader, but all I have is a partial plate.

Complete the pathfinder to reveal the missing letters in the number plate. Follow the completed pathfinder route and the correct letters will fall on the following numbers: 75, 77, 31, 91

Puzzle 38

A	D	L	S	C	B	U	R	E	T
E	H	I	T	A	R	K	C	A	T
O	T	G	H	N	I	W	F	R	O
O	B	C	S	D	T	S	O	T	R
R	D	R	A	T	L	R	O	Y	R
A	E	E	E	B	E	A	T	S	E
O	N	H	S	G	A	I	S	B	O
B	N	A	A	K	B	R	U	N	N
H	D	B	R	E	B	R	A	E	T
S	A	D	S	E	K	A	H	X	E

Parts Of A Car

Airbag, Bonnet, Boot, Brakes, Carburettor, Dashboard, Exhaust, Handbrake, Headlights, Roof Rack, Seat Belts, Tyres, Windscreen

A: _ 3 _ 4 _ 4 _

DETECTIVE MARLOWE

Well, I've got The Skeleton Key's shoe size, but not much else. I need to get a handle on this, so I decide to make a timeline of the thief's activities so far. In what order did these events occur?

Puzzle 39

A Silent alarm triggered at the Safe House Motel

B Theft reported by Queenie Royale

C Muddy footprint found at the crime scene

D Message from The Skeleton Key left at the crime scene

E Diamond stolen from the casino

F Inspector Conway tells me to file the case as unsolved

A: ....

As I review my timeline, a new case alert pings through to my work station. With a grunt of annoyance, I see that the screen on my useless old computer is playing up again. I try hitting it a few times, but I soon realise I'll have to decode the message myself. What does it say?

MESSAGE FOR DET. MARLOWE.
BREAK-IN REPORTED AT
THE CHOP SHOP.
PLEASE ATTEND.

Puzzle 40

A: ....

....

The Skeleton Key

Now that I've got the number plate, I decide to find the car and hot-wire it. I need to move fast in the car park in order to avoid suspicion – it would be good to know which space it's parked in in advance. Hmm, what number space is it?

C8A5S1S | 16 | 06 | 68 | 88 | G3T4W4Y | 98 | A1R8A6S

Puzzle 41

A: ....

I slip quietly into the car and manage to hot-wire it successfully. The mechanic will be back from his break at any moment, but I can't resist sending another message to Facade. My eye is caught by something that should do the trick perfectly.

Unjumble the letters and add the vowels to find out what it is.

Puzzle 42

A: ....

DETECTIVE MARLOWE

When I search for the address of The Chop Shop, I get two hits: a mechanics' and a butchers'. I need to narrow it down – perhaps I can find the postcode for the right business in this letter-doku?

The correct order runs from left to right.

	I				B			A
G								
	H	E		A	G		B	
			G		I	F		
	E	I				G	H	
		F	B		E			
	F		C	G		D	I	
								H
I			H				C	

A: _ _ 3 - 5 _ 7

50

Ah, I should have guessed. This business is well known to the authorities. It's run by the Throttle crime family, but I can't remember who is currently the leader. If I think carefully, I might be able to riddle it out...

The first is in wait, but not in weight.

The second is in metal, but not in mate.

The third is in checks, but not in locks.

The fourth is in ox, but not in socks.

The fifth is in iris, but not in rose.

The sixth is in does, but not in doze.

A: ....

The Skeleton Key

I can't help but laugh as I remember the look on the mechanic's face as I whizzed out of The Chop Shop in his boss' favourite car. Full of adrenaline, I head straight to my next target. It's the headquarters of a particularly powerful rival gang, and only a few people know their name.

Fill in the missing letters in these words to spell out the name of the secretive gang.

Puzzle 45

1. LOO_
2. HUS_
3. GR_ED
4. _RIBE
5. F_AUD

6. EXT_RT
7. RAC_ET
8. QUI_T
9. DI_TY
10. CA_H

A: ....

With the address of the elusive gang's headquarters programmed into the car's fancy sat nav, I cruise through the darkening streets of Vicehaven. What route do I take?

START

Puzzle 46

FINISH

DETECTIVE MARLOWE

Even for the Throttle family, Alexis has a fearsome reputation, so someone is taking a big swing if they've hit The Chop Shop. When I arrive, I find a mechanic in full panic mode – someone has stolen Alexis' beloved classic car from under his nose. He's in no state to give a statement, so I examine the tyre tracks to determine what make of car it is.

Puzzle 47

Thundercat 211

Nova Stripe

Mirage Mini

Eclipse 3000

Phantom X2

Silver Spirit

A: ....

Another personal theft targeting a high-profile criminal – this definitely feels like The Skeleton Key's MO, but without any evidence, I've got nothing to connect them to the scene. On a hunch, I compare some CCTV stills from before and after the theft. Is there anything in these images that points to The Skeleton Key's involvement?

19:54:08

20:13:48

A: ....

The Skeleton Key

The Brokers operate out of a pawn shop, but they don't exactly advertise it. As soon as I arrive at the location, I'm met with four identical doors. I know one leads to the pawn shop, one leads to the laundrette, one leads to the deli and one leads to the pet shop. Which one is the door to the pawn shop?

Puzzle 49

Door 1   Door 2   Door 3   Door 4

1. The pet shop door is surrounded on both sides.

2. The deli door is not next to the laundrette door.

3. The door to The Brokers is not a prime number.

4. The laundrette door is next to the door to The Brokers.

5. The pet shop door is not next to the door to The Brokers.

6. The business behind the first door takes weekly deliveries.

A: ....

As I approach the building, I can see the faded remains of a sign hanging over the door. By the pale moonlight, I can just about make out the shadows of the letters.

Complete the kriss kross puzzle and unjumble the circled letters to find out the official name of the headquarters.

Puzzle 50

3 letters
Arc
Awn
Bug
Era
Off
The

4 letters
Airy
Errs

5 letters
Eject
Eland
Fjord
Keels
Knife
Liege
Lunge
Owing
Putts
Rucks
Stash
Umber
Yodel

6 letters
Appeal
Hiatus
Osprey
Trifle

7 letters
Graphic
Handful
Idyllic
Inroads
Jujitsu
Ostlers

11 letters
Beautifully
Gesticulate
Gingerbread
Intelligent

A: _ _ S _ M _ _ _ _ _ U _

DETECTIVE MARLOWE

A key with a skeleton on it… a bit on the nose, but at least it confirms my suspicions. Instantly, a brilliant idea hits me.

Unjumble the circled letters to find out what it is.

A B C D E F G H I J K L M N O P Q R S T U V W X Y Z

A: _ _ _ _A_

Of course! All I need to do is hack in and I might actually be able to get ahead of The Skeleton Key for once. Luckily, my hacking skills are pretty good, and I've narrowed the access code down to these five digits. I have one more chance to enter them in the correct order before I get locked out.

Puzzle 52

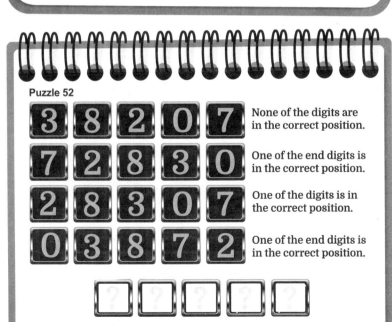

3 8 2 0 7 — None of the digits are in the correct position.

7 2 8 3 0 — One of the end digits is in the correct position.

2 8 3 0 7 — One of the digits is in the correct position.

0 3 8 7 2 — One of the end digits is in the correct position.

The Skeleton Key

I crack the two-part lock on the front door and head straight to the back office where I know the safe is. I get a thrill of excitement when I see the safe's complicated mechanism – finally, a challenge worthy of my talents! It's a bit fiddly, so I take off my gloves.

What shape is the arrow pointing at when the sequence is complete?

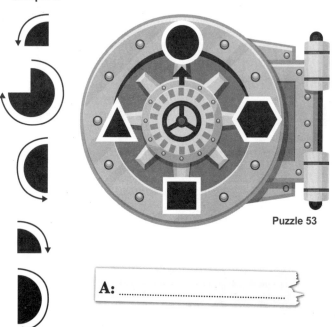

Puzzle 53

A: ....

The door pops open with the most satisfying clunk I've ever heard, revealing the safe's contents. Just like the safe at Lady Luck's, it's full to bursting with dirty money, but that's not what I reach for.

Complete the codebreaker to find out what it is.

Puzzle 54

12	26	4	21	(17)	1	24	23		2	1	12	26
6		24		24		8		22		23		18
23	26	14	5	22		8		26	22	19	2	1
3		3		15		26		10		5		2
			24	17	20	23	1	10	5	26	6	20
25		2		2		20		5		13		1
6	21	1	18	1	21		20	23	2	5	16	1
5		16		24		11		23		24		2
17	26	26	15	15	1	1	13	1	2			
17		2		5		6		1		10		12
8	6	10	1	21		7		10	24	5	11	1
1		1		7		10		24		21		16
20	5	12	1		9	24	6	21	23	5	8	3

A B C D E F G H I J K L M N O P Q R S T U V W X Y Z

1	2	3	4	5	6	7	8	9	10	11	12	13
										Z	D	

14	15	16	17	18	19	20	21	22	23	24	25	26
						S						

A: ....

DETECTIVE MARLOWE

Jackpot! I grab my keys and jump in my car.
My sat nav has shown me exactly where
The Skeleton Key is headed, and if I'm quick,
I might just catch them in the act.

I can see that the journey should take
47 minutes, but each set of traffic lights will
slow me down by 4 minutes. How long will it
take me to get there?

START

Puzzle 55

FINISH

A: ....

When I finally arrive at the location, I realise it's not going to be as easy to pinpoint my target as I'd hoped. Then, I remember that I have a photo of The Skeleton Key's footprints.

Which building have they gone to?

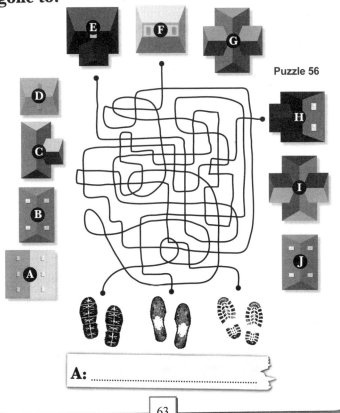

A: ....

The Skeleton Key

That's right – The Brokers' little black book is the real treasure here. I know this gift will impress Facade more than any of the others, and I can't resist a peek inside. Unsurprisingly, the names are partially written in code, but I've never encountered a code I couldn't crack.

Unscramble the first part of each name to find out who's been doing business with The Brokers.

Puzzle 57

AONRTES PATEL	£10,250
FCEIH RODRIGUEZ	£5,000
OIDRTRCE AMBROSE	£25,900
PDNSIETRE THOMPSON	£7,400
RYOMA EVANS	£12,500
EORVRNGO WANG	£8,300
PHBCHSIARO WILSON	£17,450
UEDGJ MAYFIELD	£50,000
LNECRCLOAH SINGH	£20,750
BDSMARASOA KIM	£36,500

A: ....

....

....

That's a lot of money flying around from some very powerful people. Most would argue that they're the least likely suspects for dealing with gangs like The Brokers! But what exactly are they paying for? The riddle on the back of The Brokers' business card answers that question for me.

A: ....

AS SOON AS YOU SPEAK MY NAME, I NO LONGER EXIST.

DETECTIVE MARLOWE

I make my way to the building. There's a two-part lock that obviously didn't slow down the skilled lock-pick, but it's got me stumped. Perhaps this jigsaw sudoku will reveal the first part of the code? The correct order runs from left to right.

			5					8
	9						4	
	8	2						
9			7	4		6		
8				3	◯			4
		7		9	6			3
						1	5	
	3		◯				9	◯
1		◯			4			

A: ....

The first part of the lock deactivates and I get a buzz of satisfaction – I can see how this could get addictive.
For the second part, I need to work out the password. Luckily, I know a little bit about this brand of lock.

- I know the password must spell out the name of a planet in our solar system.
- I know I can only press each number key once.
- What numbers do I press to enter the password?

Puzzle 60

A: ....

The Skeleton Key

I can hear someone tinkering with the lock on the front door – surely no one else would be able to crack it? But I can't help feeling nervous, so it's time for me to get out of here. I want to leave one final message for Facade. To do so, I need to take exactly £613,145 from the safe.

Which stacks of cash should I take?

Puzzle 61

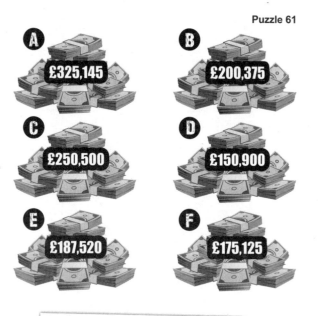

A £325,145

B £200,375

C £250,500

D £150,900

E £187,520

F £175,125

A: ....

I stuff the stacks in my backpack just as I hear the electronic chime of the lock deactivating. Panicking, I look around for a way out. With seconds to spare, I spot my best option. What is it?

Puzzle 62

A: ....

DETECTIVE MARLOWE

The lock releases and, heart thumping, I make my way to the back office. The Skeleton Key has clearly just left in a hurry – they've dropped their gloves by the safe in their haste. They must have gone through the emergency exit, but the signs on the doors are all mixed up. I know only one of the signs can be labelled correctly – which door will lead me outside?

Door 1

Door 2

Door 3

Puzzle 63

A: ....

Gasping for breath, I burst through the door and race across the street. Just as my eyes are adjusting to the darkness, I'm blinded by a sudden bright light. Where is it coming from?

Puzzle 64

	14		15		22		15		2		5	
17	22	19	9	11	16	22	8	3	2	3	20	
	10		26		2		20		13		18	
10	11	19	24		21	22	20	7	26	9	2	13
		2		2		25		3		4	
5	15	11	6	11	15	15		26	21	22	4	9
	9		2		11		20		11		11	
1	5	11	15	9		4	19	11	15	2	21	11
	7		26		12		26		13			
26	24	15	9	19	26	13	9		11	9	13	12
	6		2		6		2		3		26	
19	11	13	22	2	6		23	26	13	2	6	11
	21		3		15		25		11		6	

A B C D E F G H I J K L M N O P Q R S T U V W X Y Z

1	2	3	4	5	6	7	8	9	10	11	12	13
								T		E		

14	15	16	17	18	19	20	21	22	23	24	25	26
		X										

A: ....

71

The Skeleton Key

Jumping in the car, I see a silhouette standing in the street – is this who has been on my tail? I slam my foot on the accelerator and squeal past them. Though I soon realise I need to slow down – the last thing I need is to be caught speeding. I don't know this part of the city – what's the speed limit around here?

Complete the sudoku and add up the circled numbers to find out.

					2			5
5						3	8	
			5	8		1		
	7		9				3	
8			7		3			9
	3				4		5	
	1		8	6				
	8	6						7
9			5					

A: ....

As I roll through the streets of Vicehaven, I wonder... how did my mysterious pursuer know where to find me? My stomach drops as I realise this car must have a tracking system. I need to pull over and log in to the car's onboard system to disable it, fast!

Find the speed-themed password by travelling to each circle along the lines. You can only use each circle once.

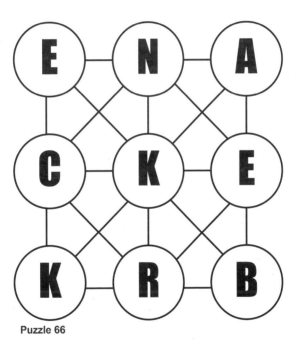

Puzzle 66

A: ....

DETECTIVE MARLOWE

I leap out of the way just in time as the Phantom X2 speeds off into the night. I've no hope of catching up in my police-issued rust bucket, so head back inside to gather as much evidence as I can. On the ground, a torn up sheet of paper catches my eye.

What order should the pieces be in?

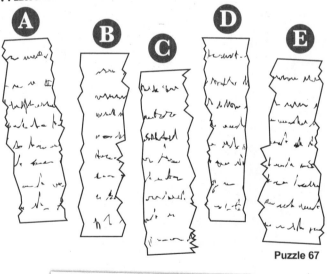

Puzzle 67

A: ....

This piece of paper has turned out to be quite revealing indeed. Not only did it give me the name of this business – Hush Money Hut – but it also detailed exactly how much money should be in the safe tonight.

Complete the brain chain to find out how much money is actually in the safe. The correct amount is a six-figure sum.

Puzzle 68

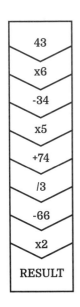

43
x6
-34
x5
+74
/3
-66
x2
RESULT

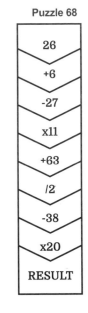

26
+6
-27
x11
+63
/2
-38
x20
RESULT

A: ....

The Skeleton Key

Safely back at home, all I can do is wait. I've hit each one of Facade's rivals, I can only hope that my messages were received. To pass the time, I whizz through the puzzle pages of today's Vicehaven Herald, but one seems to be pointing me to another section in the newspaper...

Unjumble the circled letters to find out where to look next.

Puzzle 69

ABCDEFGHIJKLMNOPQRSTUVWXYZ

A: ....

I flick to the back of the newspaper and scan the brightly coloured notices. One rather peculiar advert catches my eye. I know a coded message when I see one. What does it say?

Puzzle 70

WEDNESDAY EVENINGS

Luna's lively dancefloor open now! Excited to sing karaoke? Get online today, or ring our switchboard. Experience beautiful, unforgettable delights from Luna's only!

RELAX IN STYLE TONIGHT!

A: ....

DETECTIVE MARLOWE

Back at the VPD, The Skeleton Key's trail has gone cold. They disabled the Phantom X2's sat nav, so there's no way of tracking where they are. Frustrated, I make a list of everything I know so far.

Tick 'true' or 'false' next to each statement.

	T	F
The Skeleton Key left their fingerprints at two scenes.	......	......
Queenie Royale and Alexis Throttle are connected to criminal gangs.	......	......
A diamond and cash were taken from Queenie Royale's safe.	......	......
The Skeleton Key must have walked to Hush Money Hut.	......	......
Alex Throttle operates out of The Chop Shop.	......	......
The Skeleton Key is connected to an unsolved kidnapping.	......	......
The Clean-up Crew is implicated in a theft from Vicehaven Gallery.	......	......
The Skeleton Key has size 9 feet.	......	......

Puzzle 71

Instinctively, I check the logs to see if any break-ins have been reported, but there's nothing. Maybe I'm being too impatient, it hasn't been that long since the break-in at Hush Money Hut after all...

Complete the puzzle by visiting each square once, starting at 1 and ending at 100, to find out how many hours it's been since The Skeleton Key's last appearance.

Puzzle 72

	4			46					51
		8			59	58		53	
1		44						56	
			99		85		80		
11		63		100	97	96	84		
							78	75	
	⃝	40		91	92				71
		38				68			
	18	35	34		32		30		
16				21		23		25	

A: ....

The Skeleton Key

I'm almost certain the message in the paper is from Facade, but I'm still cautious as I approach the counter at Rosebud Florist. I ask the assistant if there are any deliveries to be collected. He grunts and presents me with three bunches of flowers for three different recipients and asks which ones are for me.

KEELEY
KATH STONE

ETHEL
TOKENSKY

THEO KELSEY
KENT

Puzzle 73

A: ....

He hands me the bunch of flowers, and I can see there's a small card nestled in the stems. I pick it out carefully – it's a tiny anagram. I have a feeling this will point me in the direction of my next message.

Unjumble the letters to find the next location.

Puzzle 74

A: ....

DETECTIVE MARLOWE

Time to process the evidence I took from Hush Money Hut. Upon seeing the gloves on the floor, I was pretty confident I could get a fingerprint for The Skeleton Key this time. I dusted the whole place and there was only one set of fingerprints on the safe. Which one was it?

Puzzle 75

SAMPLE A

SAMPLE B

SAMPLE C

SAMPLE D

SAMPLE E

SAMPLE F

SAMPLE G

SAMPLE H

A: ....

This must be The Skeleton Key's print.
I run it through the database and get
matches for a raft of other unsolved
crimes. It would almost be quicker to list
the crimes they *haven't* been involved in...

The crime that doesn't appear in the
wordsearch is one that The Skeleton Key
hasn't been connected to.

Puzzle 76

V	P	E	S	Q	T	R	Y	D	Y	J	L	B	R
P	I	H	H	C	X	H	F	R	A	U	D	R	F
S	C	R	O	P	L	T	E	V	V	J	M	I	Q
T	K	B	P	D	A	G	A	F	P	P	M	B	G
N	P	S	L	O	R	Q	O	D	T	N	J	E	Y
R	O	B	I	O	C	E	D	T	O	K	Y	R	A
H	C	S	F	G	E	K	I	I	W	R	E	Y	B
D	K	W	T	X	N	J	T	O	A	B	X	Q	U
D	E	T	I	W	Y	R	F	L	B	J	U	J	J
P	T	D	N	O	O	F	G	O	B	U	Q	F	S
G	I	S	G	T	T	R	R	L	U	F	G	Q	E
K	N	W	X	Q	U	H	A	F	T	X	Y	K	H
O	G	E	M	B	E	Z	Z	L	E	M	E	N	T
B	G	X	J	R	H	U	Q	Z	J	F	S	Q	H

Bribery	Shoplifting	Forgery	Pickpocketing
Extortion	Burglary	Robbery	Kidnapping
Theft	Embezzlement	Fraud	Larceny

A: ....

83

The Skeleton Key

Flowers in hand, I leave Rosebud Florist. As luck would have it, there's a bus stop opposite, and as I watch, the bus that goes via the train station pulls up. I pay my fare, give the flowers to the lovely driver, and take my seat.

Follow the bus journey through Vicehaven to the train station.

START

Puzzle 77

FINISH

I hop off the bus at Vicehaven Central, but I don't really know where to go next. Just as I'm looking around for a clue, someone bumps into me. They say nothing, but as they walk away, I notice something has been slipped into my pocket. What is it?

BF OI RA NS DT

MC EL AR SP SK

TL HR EA ID NY

GT UI DC KA ER TN

Puzzle 78

A: ....

DETECTIVE MARLOWE

There's something different that's bothering me about the last crime scene, but I can't pin it down. I decide to take a little break with a newspaper puzzle. Unjumble the circled letters to get a nudge in the right direction.

Puzzle 79

3 letters
Ell
Not
Phi
Pro
Red
Yen
Yes

4 letters
Arid
Done
Dyed
Each
Ever
Gust
Leer
Menu
Onyx
Vice

5 letters
Ennui
Sedan

6 letters
Nearby
Notate

7 letters
Actuate
Alleged
Gleeful
Languor
Naively
Realist
Sucking
Unbound

8 letters
Confetti
Operetta
Reverted
Seascape

9 letters
Detective
Explosion

A: ....

That's it! I thought it was strange, as it didn't seem to fit The Skeleton Key's MO. Thanks to the piece of paper I found, I know there was supposed to be £1,289,565 in the safe last night, and I know how much was actually in there. So how much did The Skeleton Key take?

....

Could The Skeleton Key have taken this strangely specific amount to send a message? If so, what could the numbers represent?

....

Puzzle 80

A: ....

The Skeleton Key

I step onto the train and try to find my seat. This is my first time in first class, and the seat numbering system is bizarre, to say the least. Which one is my seat?

Row:		Seat:		
A			3	6
				12
G				
			27	
Q				
	→			

Puzzle 81

A: ....

I take my seat, and before long, the conductor comes by and asks for my ticket. I hand it over and he stamps and returns it, but he passes me something else at the same time.

Unjumble the letters to find out what it is.

Puzzle 82

A: ....

DETECTIVE MARLOWE

Aha! Could this be the breakthrough I've been hoping for? I run the alias 'Facade' through the system and get a hit on another name that sounds familiar to me.

Each of these crime-themed anagrams has one extra letter. The extra letters make the name connected to Facade.

Puzzle 83

....
VELCRTID

....
HAILIB

....
AVEITUTSGINE

....
TLIYTUG

....
RNYUJ

....
ENFIGRPTIRCN

....
WLAA

....
ASFUHCDLNF

....
NDEINCEEV

....
TEEUITEVDC

....
IWSSEITN

....
EOLBVS

....
TCUGPSSE

A: ....

My heart drops when I realise where I know that name from – it's rumoured to be the haunt of Vicehaven's most fearsome gang. Suddenly, all the pieces start to come together.

Match the puzzle pieces to find the name of each gang name, headquarters and leader.

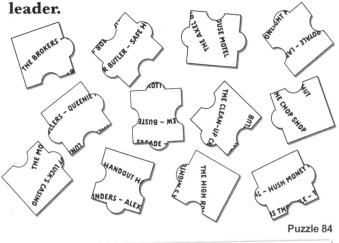

THE BROKERS

R BUTLER – SAFE H

USE MOTEL
THE AXE

OYALE – LA

LERS – QUEENIE

EW – BUSTE

THE CLEAN-UP C

E CHOP SHOP

THE M

LUCK'S CASINO

HANDOUT H

NDERS – ALEX

S RIGHT

THE HIGH R

– HUSH MONE

IS TH

Puzzle 84

A:
1. ....
2. ....
3. ....
4. ....
5. ....

91

The Skeleton Key

I turn on the burner phone and it asks me for a passcode. I smile as I settle in to crack the code – I'm back in my comfort zone for the first time since I stepped into this first class carriage.

Complete the sudoku to find the passcode. The correct order runs from left to right.

◯	2	5			7	4		
		2						6
	4	5			6	3		
			6		◯		9	3
		3		5				
1	7	◯		8				
		7	1			9	3	◯
4					2			
	3	9			4	2		

Puzzle 85

A: ....

92

Immediately, a message alert pings.

Congratulations to The Skeleton Key.
We are most impressed with your feats so far.
There is something big on the horizon, and we'd
like you to play a starring role. First, we need you to
purloin a few extra. Head to the following location
and keep an eye out for further instructions.

☾

YARBILR

I can't believe it, the Moonlight Mob are asking
me to help with 'something big' – I must really
have impressed them! First, I just need to work
out where they're sending me...

A: ....

DETECTIVE MARLOWE

That's it! The only criminal gang in Vicehaven The Skeleton Key hasn't hit is the Moonlight Mob. I can only assume this cocky thief is auditioning for Facade, and I don't like the idea of these criminal factions teaming up. It's time to take this to top brass – my boss, Inspector Conway. In an abundance of caution, I send the message in code. What does it say? Puzzle 87

> Irs,
> I aveh easonr ot elieveb hist atestl pates fo rimesc si het orkw fo a ewn layerp ithw onnectionsc ot het Oonlightm Obm. Ermissionp ot ormf a opt ecrets askt orcef ot nvestigatei?

A: ....

....

....

....

....

I begin to gather up all my evidence so far, but within seconds, I get a reply from Conway. He's written back in code, although a slightly different one to mine. What is he ordering me to do?

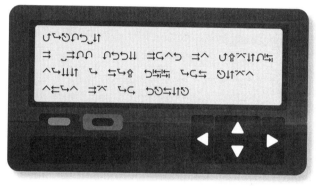

↳	⇄	⤵	⇆	↕	⇶	↥	⇇
A	B	C	D	E	F	G	H

⇉	⇈	⇊	⋂	↺	↶	↻	↺
I	J	K	L	M	N	O	P

↺	↻	⤬	∧	⤛	⌣	⌣	⇧
Q	R	S	T	U	V	W	X

⇧	⇦
Y	Z

A: ....

The Skeleton Key

Of all the places I was expecting the Moonlight Mob to send me, the library definitely wasn't one of them. But I'm intrigued nonetheless. I check the train map and try to remember which stop is for the library. Perhaps this kriss kross puzzle can jog my memory.

3 letters
Our
Use

4 letters
Evil
Onto

5 letters
Again
China
Edges
Grail
Idyll
Lapel
Lease
Raise
Sassy
Sweep

6 letters
Airman
Assign
Chorus
Coccyx
Nurses
Unpack

7 letters
Amphora
Yelling

8 letters
Exertion
Macaroni

11 letters
Amorousness
Maliciously
Principally
Significant
Unrelenting
Variability

A: _ E _ _ N _ _ _ A _ _

Despite all the excitement, a wave of exhaustion suddenly washes over me, and I wonder if I'll have time for a quick nap before we get there. I know my train left Vicehaven Central at 14:58. I also know it's exactly 8 minutes between each stop, and the train spends 90 seconds at each stop. At what time will I arrive at my stop?

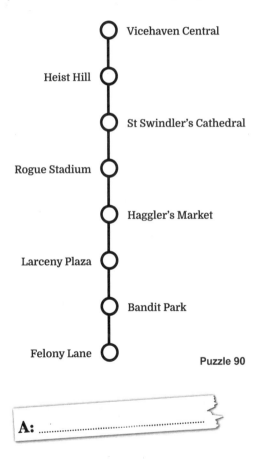

Vicehaven Central

Heist Hill

St Swindler's Cathedral

Rogue Stadium

Haggler's Market

Larceny Plaza

Bandit Park

Felony Lane

Puzzle 90

A: ....

DETECTIVE MARLOWE

I admit I am pretty tired, so I head down to the front desk to clock out for the day. I can't resist taking a police scanner with me though – I don't want to miss it if The Skeleton Key strikes again. All I need to do is turn it to the correct frequency. Complete the jigsaw sudoku to find the frequency. The correct order runs from left to right.

Puzzle 91

3	6							
	4	7					1	
2	◯	1		3				4
	7	◯	6		4	8		
◯		◯						
		4	5		7		3	
6				2		1	◯	5
	3					9	6	◯
					◯		2	3

A: _ _ _ - _ _ _ MHz

It's a beautiful, bright day, so I take a stroll through the city to try and clear my head.

Complete the wordsearch to discover what I see on my stroll through Vicehaven.

P	L	Z	I	O	B	P	K	U	L	A	V	R	O	S
M	S	L	A	N	E	R	A	T	I	W	K	A	W	T
T	P	P	J	U	I	E	J	C	O	T	T	A	G	E
Y	F	E	P	B	D	B	F	O	R	T	R	E	S	S
M	H	A	O	M	O	N	A	S	T	E	R	Y	A	T
M	T	R	W	O	S	A	N	C	H	X	S	E	C	A
O	B	S	E	R	V	A	T	O	R	Y	M	O	V	B
A	A	Y	R	P	U	B	U	H	I	U	L	U	A	L
E	R	R	S	A	A	S	K	C	O	L	M	O	D	E
D	N	D	T	U	E	R	J	U	E	U	I	K	O	K
A	X	S	A	A	B	G	C	G	F	R	S	V	G	B
C	H	A	T	E	A	U	E	S	I	L	O	E	A	S
B	L	L	I	M	D	N	I	W	Y	D	G	O	P	P
E	S	U	O	H	T	H	G	I	L	K	E	Y	I	O
N	T	T	N	J	N	M	U	E	L	O	S	U	A	M

ARENA	FORTRESS	POWER STATION
BARN	LIGHTHOUSE	PUB
BOATHOUSE	MAUSOLEUM	SILO
CABIN	MONASTERY	SKYSCRAPER
CHATEAU	OBSERVATORY	STABLE
COLLEGE	PAGODA	WAREHOUSE
COTTAGE	PAVILION	WINDMILL

99

The Skeleton Key

Feeling refreshed after a short nap, I stroll into the library and look around the foyer. One wall is covered in artsy word posters. I wonder if this is where the Moonlight Mob might leave me a message...

One of these words is the odd one out. The others can all be turned into new words by adding the same word. Which is the odd word out?

Puzzle 93

A: ....

After figuring that out, and checking that the coast is clear, I gently peel back the strange poster and see a piece of paper is lodged behind it. I pull it loose and it flutters to the ground. Let me see... it's a riddle, and the answer must be telling me where to go next, if only I can work it out...

Puzzle 94

Where does Friday come before Thursday?

A: ....

DETECTIVE MARLOWE

My feet have brought me to Vicehaven Library.
I know the library's news archives will be a great
place to read up on the Moonlight Mob. I walk in,
sit at a desk and try to remember my username.
Complete the A – Z to find the username.
The correct order runs from left to right.

Puzzle 95

D	E	C	◯		A	T	E	█	S	◯	O	P
I	█	H	E		U		I	█	E			
P	L	A				◯	U	D	G	E		
S				E		D				S		
█			U	A	◯	R	I	C	E	P	S	
	C		R		O	█		R	█	M		
O	R	A	◯	E	D	█	D	I	P	O	L	E
Y		U		M	E		D	◯		N		
S	U	C	C	E	S	S		U	L	█		
T		U		N		C		A		I	T	
I	N	S		T	◯		L	I	N	E	R	
		E		S		D			T	E		
K	I	S	S	█		O	D		W	◯	R	

A B C D E F G H I J K L M N O P Q R S T U V W X Y Z

A: ....

Well, my username was accepted, but the password I tried was wrong. Luckily, I set up a forgotten password hint. Surely I can work it out from this?

Find the password by travelling to each circle along the lines. You can only use each circle once.

Hint: your favourite Gothic novel.

A: ....

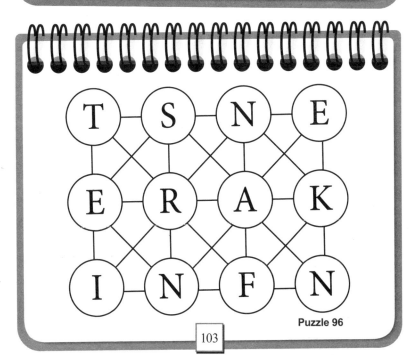

Puzzle 96

103

The Skeleton Key

I head over to the reference section where the library's giant dictionary sits on a plinth. There are hundreds of pages, where do I start? A scrap of paper poking out from under the book might give me a clue...

Fill in the missing numbers to find the correct page number in the grey hexagon.

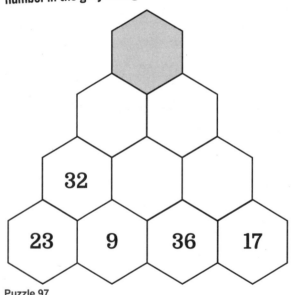

Puzzle 97

A: ....

I turn to the right page and scan it for clues. Scribbled in the margin is a series of numbers. A light bulb goes on in my head when I realise what it is.

Unjumble the circled letters below to find out.

Puzzle 98

1	2	3	4	5	6	7	8	9	10	11	12	13
												W

14	15	16	17	18	19	20	21	22	23	24	25	26
J	A											

A: ....

105

DETECTIVE MARLOWE

Finally logged in, I click through to the historical archives and search for all news stories that mention the words 'moonlight' and 'mob'. Instantly, my screen is flooded with search results! Complete the sudoku to find out how many there are. The correct order runs from left to right.

		3	2		1			8
				8	4	◯		6
			3			9		
3	7						9	◯
	1		7		5		6	
	2			◯			4	1
◯		9			3			
1	◯		8	2				
6			1		9	3		

Puzzle 99

A: ....

Okay, that's way too many. I need to narrow this down, so I decide to filter my search by keywords. I can only include a maximum of 10 keywords, but which ones to choose?

The two words that don't appear in the wordsearch are not included in the keywords.

Puzzle 100

D	E	A	L	I	N	G	S	F	C	L	U	V	M
S	C	N	W	H	E	N	C	H	M	E	N	Y	C
F	L	I	T	L	Q	G	B	I	L	O	T	A	A
Q	A	F	U	E	M	B	J	N	I	J	O	Q	F
Y	N	X	W	I	R	Q	O	T	X	P	U	F	E
W	D	C	B	A	O	P	P	I	B	P	C	I	A
V	E	O	S	H	V	U	R	M	Q	F	H	N	W
V	S	N	H	D	R	C	K	I	S	A	A	A	C
L	T	V	W	R	M	X	C	D	S	A	B	N	F
X	I	I	O	R	W	T	Q	A	X	E	L	C	O
Y	N	C	R	I	M	E	Z	T	U	B	E	I	E
F	E	T	M	G	Q	C	U	I	P	G	T	A	A
A	A	E	N	L	P	A	Y	O	F	F	H	L	N
X	D	D	U	Q	E	B	D	N	O	U	X	T	A

Caught	Corruption	Enterprise	Intimidation
Clandestine	Convicted	Financial	Payoff
Convicted	Dealings	Henchmen	Untouchable

A: ....

The Skeleton Key

I know that the cipher will tell me where to find each letter of a hidden message. I'm about to get started, but the librarian announces over the tannoy that they will be closing soon. How many minutes do I have to work out the cipher?

I'm an odd number, but if you take away one of my letters, I become even. What am I?

A: ....

Quick, I must figure out the cipher to decode the message on the page. It seems to be spelling out a name. What is it?

Puzzle 102

A: N _ _ E _ _ AR _ ER

DETECTIVE MARLOWE

That's a much more manageable list of articles.
I start to make detailed notes on all the crime stories
connected to the Moonlight Mob to see if I can find
any new patterns.

Follow the train of thought through the maze to see
what comes up.

START

Puzzle 103

FINISH

A: ....

While a useful observation, that's nothing myself or the VPD didn't already know. With a frustrated sigh, I take a gulp of my tepid coffee. What am I missing?

Starting in the top left, join the hexagons by creating a new word that's only one letter different from the last. Each hexagon must connect to exactly two adjacent hexagons. The word in the grey hexagons is the answer.

A: ....

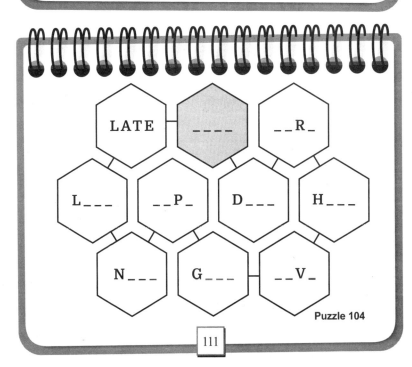

LATE   _ _ _ _   _ _ R _

L _ _ _   _ _ P _   D _ _ _   H _ _ _

N _ _ _   G _ _ _   _ _ V _

Puzzle 104

The Skeleton Key

That's got to be an author's name, right? I scan the shelves for Niles Carter, but I come up empty. I search the whole library, but I can't find this author anywhere. Just as I'm about to give up, I spot a sign for a section I hadn't seen before.

Unjumble the letters to find out what it is. Every other letter is missing.

Puzzle 105

A: _ _ _ _   _ _ _ _ _

Whatever's in here, it's obviously super valuable because the door to get into the temperature-controlled room is locked – as if *that* could stop me.

I assess the alphanumerical keypad on the lock. I know the numbers spell out a day of the week and that each button can only be pressed once. What numbers do I press?

A: ....

DETECTIVE MARLOWE

Hmm... I've never really looked that closely at the dates before, but it's worth a quick search. I carefully type all the dates of all the crimes connected to the Moonlight Mob in the last six months into the archive search bar.

Complete the sums to fill in the missing month in each date. Remember to add a zero in front of any single-digit numbers.

Puzzle 107

$$48 \div 6 = 21/\_\_$$
$$30 - 13 - 8 - 5 = 23/\_\_$$
$$54 \div 2 \div 3 = 20/\_\_$$
$$44 - 12 - 19 - 7 = 22/\_\_$$
$$70 \div 5 \div 2 = 22/\_\_$$
$$100 \div 4 \div 5 = 23/\_\_$$

I hit enter and – much to my surprise – I get a perfect hit on a news story from only last month. Based on the information in the article, what will be the name of the next full moon?

Vicehaven Herald

MOON-THLY FUN FOR STARGAZERS

Ron Waffle

If you go up to Heist Hill tonight, you may be in for a surprise. You won't find any bears, but you may well find a picnic or two as local stargazers gather to observe tonight's full moon. These lunar lovers have turned their hobby into a monthly tradition, meeting on Heist Hill once a month with telescopes, snacks and blankets to keep them warm as they enjoy the spectacle.

The group's founder, Celeste Sparks, says the gatherings are about more than astronomy.

"It's a wonderful way to connect with our community and appreciate the beauty of the night sky," she explains. "We share stories, learn about the stars and just enjoy some peace and quiet – which isn't always easy to find in Vicehaven!"

Last month's Sturgeon Moon gathering even featured a guest appearance by local musician Tyler Drift, who serenaded the group with moon-themed tunes.

If you're interested in taking part, here's a list of this year's full moons:

January 25 Wolf Moon
February 24 Snow Moon
March 25 Worm Moon
April 23 Pink Moon
May 23 Flower Moon
June 22 Strawberry Moon
July 22 Buck Moon
August 21 Sturgeon Moon
September 20 Corn Moon
October 20 Hunter's Moon
November 18 Beaver Moon
December 19 Cold Moon

So, next time the moon is full, wrap up warm and head to Heist Hill. There's nothing quite like the magic of a full moon to bring the best and brightest of Vicehaven out to shine.

Puzzle 108

A: ....

115

The Skeleton Key

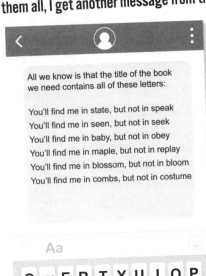

Bingo! I slip inside and immediately locate a whole block of books by Niles Carter. Just as I'm wondering if I should take them all, I get another message from the Moonlight Mob.

All we know is that the title of the book we need contains all of these letters:

You'll find me in state, but not in speak
You'll find me in seen, but not in seek
You'll find me in baby, but not in obey
You'll find me in maple, but not in replay
You'll find me in blossom, but not in bloom
You'll find me in combs, but not in costume

Which letters am I looking for?

Puzzle 109

A: ....

Well, that certainly narrows it down. I kneel down to examine the titles more closely and find the one that contains all those letters.

Which one is it?

Puzzle 110

A: ....

117

DETECTIVE MARLOWE

Of course! The Moonlight Mob only commits crimes on a full moon, how did I not see this before? I pick up my radio to call Inspector Conway but stop myself. He gets very prickly if people contact him when he's off duty. If it's past 5:30pm, I'll have to radio the head of the Organised Crime Unit, Anne Bush, instead.

Puzzle 111

I clocked out of the VPD at 15:38.
It took me 29 minutes to walk to the library.
Once I got to the library, I went to the bathroom, which took 4 minutes.
I've been in the archives ever since, and according to my library account, I've been online for 87 minutes.

Who should I call?

A: ....

I can't make a call in here – lest I incur the wrath of the librarian – so I gather my things to step outside. First, there's something I want to check. I bring up the astronomical charts to see when the next full moon is.

Unjumble the circled letters to find out.

Puzzle 112

	I	L	D		I						R	N
			O		N		N		E		O	
R	E	V	E	R	T		S	Y	N	T	A	
	B		R		E	M					S	
C	A	N	S		R		E		E	C	(○)	S
	N				I				N			
	A	D	I	U			B	L	E	N		
		M					U				U	
(○)	Y	M		(○)	S		(○)			I	S	A
	O		E		I	V			O		T	
	U	O	T	E	D		A		C	E	P	T
	N		U		E		N		A		A	
E	G	G	S		S	E	T	T	L	(○)	N	(○)

A B C D E F G H I J K L M N O P Q R S T U V W X Y Z

A: _ _ _ _ _ _ _ T

The Skeleton Key

I pull out my burner phone to let the Moonlight Mob know I've successfully tracked down the book, but there's already a new message waiting with my next instructions.

Each of these library-themed anagrams has one extra letter. The extra letters reveal where I should go next.

IETUTQ	SEFHEVLS
HINXDE	RRBFOWO
ARBIIALREN	NRLERA
PUCLSIB	SEROIOTS
MTVLEOU	TAOCUGLAEO
OSAOBK	OKGDEMLWEN

Puzzle 113

A: ....

Not what I was expecting, but then again, this whole day has been a turn up for the books. I leave the rare books room and hear the heavy door clunk shut behind me as I make my way towards the lifts. When I step inside, I notice the labels next to the buttons have all fallen off.

Which floor do I need to go to?

Puzzle 114

5

4

3

2

1

Restaurant / Children's books / Gift shop

Fiction A–M / Fiction N–Z / Quiet zone

Non-fiction / Reference / Staff room

Rare books / Archives / Reading room

Reception / Information / Security

A: ....

DETECTIVE MARLOWE

My heart is racing. Could the Moonlight Mob and The Skeleton Key be planning an audacious crime tonight?

At that moment, the librarian, Shirley Shushman, bustles over to me. She follows a strict no-talking policy, so she hands me a note written in her librarian shorthand. What does it say?

Puzzle 115

A: ....

....

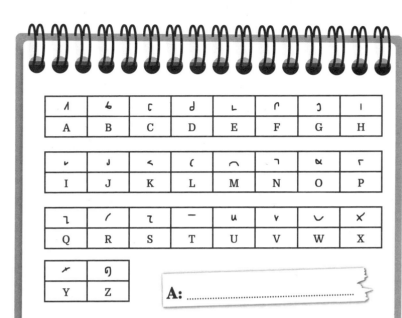

∧	ᒥ	ᐸ	d	ᒪ	⌒	⊃	I
A	B	C	D	E	F	G	H

✔	⌐	⋖	⟨	⌒	⌐	∝	⌐
I	J	K	L	M	N	O	P

⌐	⟋	⟋	⁻	⋃	∨	⌣	✕
Q	R	S	T	U	V	W	X

⟋	⟍
Y	Z

A: ....

I'm not technically on duty, and I'm anxious to share what I've discovered about the Moonlight Mob, but I agree to take a quick look. Which of the following messages do I scribble back to Shirley?

A ꝛ⟋⟋⟋✕ ✔ ∧⌒ ⌐⟋⁻ ⟋∧ ⟋ᵁ⁻✕

B ✔ ∧⌒ ⌐⟋⁻ ⟋ᒪ⁻ᒪᒪ⁻ᵂᵁᒪ ⌒∧⟋⟋⟋∧⌣ᒪ

C ⟋ᒪ ᒪ⟋ᵁ⟋⟋ᒪ ✔ ∧⌒ ✔∧⟋⟋✕ ⁻⟋ ᒪᒪᒪ

The Skeleton Key

The rickety lift shudders to a stop and I step out onto Floor 2. I make straight for the staff room without being spotted. At the door, I'm see a keypad with a five-digit code and I must admit, I'm pleased to be back in the realm of numbers and lock-picking.

What's the code to get into the staff room?

Puzzle 117

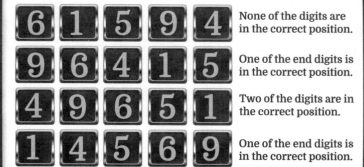

6	1	5	9	4	None of the digits are in the correct position.
9	6	4	1	5	One of the end digits is in the correct position.
4	9	6	5	1	Two of the digits are in the correct position.
1	4	5	6	9	One of the end digits is in the correct position.

I push the door open and shuffle into the stuffy room. Fortunately, there's no one in here, but there doesn't seem to be anything worth stealing in here either. I scan the room – where would anything valuable be kept in a room like this?

Unjumble the circled letters to find out.

Puzzle 118

A B C D E F G H I J K L M N O P Q R S T U V W X Y Z

A: ....

DETECTIVE MARLOWE

I follow Shirley to the rare books room, but instead of going inside, she opens a control panel hidden next to the door. I realise the door must have automatically locked when the silent alarm was triggered, so the first thing I need to do is reset it.

Which wire do I need to pull out?

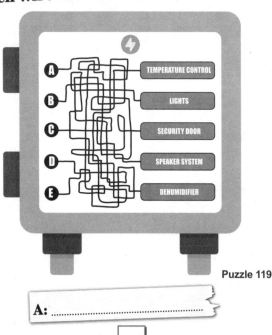

A — TEMPERATURE CONTROL
B — LIGHTS
C — SECURITY DOOR
D — SPEAKER SYSTEM
E — DEHUMIDIFIER

Puzzle 119

A: ....

I disconnect the alarm and the door resets with a click. We push our way inside and I look around while Shirley takes out her scanner and conducts a rapid inventory. Which ISBN is missing?

6	2	9	7	8	1	6	3	5	3	4	6	7	8	0
6	7	3	7	4	6	8	9	2	7	2	9	1	7	0
9	3	9	0	5	4	2	2	8	7	6	7	8	7	9
7	7	7	7	1	2	7	9	7	5	5	8	8	7	7
8	8	8	3	8	8	8	1	6	6	3	1	8	7	4
1	9	1	5	6	8	2	6	5	6	2	6	8	7	9
8	7	6	9	8	8	9	5	2	8	6	8	2	0	1
6	0	7	6	9	7	6	8	4	7	3	4	7	6	6
7	9	8	8	1	5	7	7	2	5	3	6	2	5	7
4	2	2	5	2	0	9	8	7	7	6	6	8	7	9
5	5	2	0	8	9	4	3	2	3	9	4	4	5	0
5	6	4	7	8	2	3	1	8	2	4	2	9	8	0
7	7	5	3	1	4	2	6	1	3	0	3	6	8	6
8	7	0	6	7	8	2	4	3	3	1	8	7	9	7
6	9	9	7	8	1	2	3	9	8	5	6	6	3	2

9781867455786   9784331702649   9781684664238

9781635346780   9781334287607   9752862736486

9787678224509   9788982792692   9786265628651

9786677890252   9786672842169   9781678224509

9781239856632   9776529079873

A: ....

The Skeleton Key

I turn to the wall of lockers. They seem pretty secure, and I can't wait to get stuck into picking another lock – as soon as I can work out which locker I need. Right on cue, a ping announces the arrival of another cryptic clue on my phone.

Work out which numbers from 1 – 9 fit into each box. Each number can only be used once. The numbers in the circles reveal the correct answer, and run left to right.

Puzzle 121

(○)	+		–		=3
x		+		–	
	+		x	(○)	=9
–		–		–	
	–	(○)	–		=2
=1		=9		=4	

A: ....

I'm pretty confident this is the right locker, but the lock mechanism is like nothing I've ever seen before.

Work out what number each shape represents to find the combination to open the locker.

$$\triangle + \diamondsuit = 6$$

$$\square \times \triangle = 12$$

$$\bigcirc - \square = 2$$

$$\diamondsuit \times \bigcirc = 10$$

$$\bigcirc \times \triangle = 20$$

Combination: $\triangle$ $\square$ $\bigcirc$ $\diamondsuit$

Puzzle 122

A: ....

DETECTIVE MARLOWE

The missing ISBN is part of a batch of books that has only just arrived. There's no title or author name, but there is a Dewey Decimal code.

Complete the sudoku to fill in the numbers of the code. The correct order runs from left to right.

5			6			◯	2	
	9	6	◯	5				
	3		4					9
6	4	3			1		◯	
		7				4		◯
		◯	2			3	7	6
9					2		3	
			5			6	4	
	8		◯		6			1

A: _ _ _ - _ _ _

I've spent enough time in the library to know what historical subject area those first three digits denote.

Unjumble the letters and insert some vowels to discover the subject area.

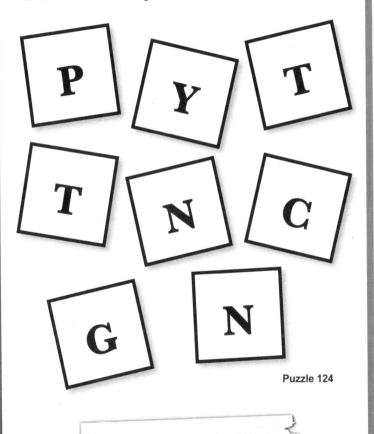

P **Y** **T**

T **N** **C**

G **N**

Puzzle 124

A: _ _ _ _ _ _ _   _ _ _ _ _

The Skeleton Key

The locker door pops open to reveal a whole heap of... junk. It's packed with papers, old food wrappers and the odd smelly sock. What on earth could the Moonlight Mob want in here? As if they could read my thoughts, they send another coded message.

Complete the letter-doku below. The letters in the circles reveal the correct answer, and run left to right.

Puzzle 125

	○			G		C	E	
			E					F
		A		I	F		B	
		D		F				
B	C		○				F	I
				B		H		
	A		B	H		D		○
H					D			
D	B		I					

A: ....

I gingerly pick through the rubbish until I find the item in question. Just as I pull it out, I hear a noise at the door – someone's coming in! I whip behind a pile of boxes and watch in horror as a security guard walks in and goes straight to locker 541. They soon realise that something's been taken and rush back out of the room. I'm thinking now would be a good time to leave the library, but the Moonlight Mob has one final cryptic quest for me. Where am I going next?

Go back to where you were before.
To a different room but the very same floor.
You'll need to move with stealth and speed.
You're there to search and not to read.

A: ....

DETECTIVE MARLOWE

Strangely, the only other information available about the stolen book on the library system is a scan of an old letter from the author. It looks like it was written on an old typewriter with a few broken keys.

Work out which three letters are missing to read the note.

```
It has b___ ma_y y_a_s of
s_a_chi_g, but I hav_ fi_ally
__t_i_v_d th_ fam_d _m__ald _y_
of Ho_us. _o o__ b_li_v_d m_ wh__
I said I would fi_d it. I_ this
book is th_ only __co_d of this
p_ic_l_ss a_t_fact to b_ fou_d
a_ywh___ i_ th_ wo_ld.
```

A: ....

134

Curiouser and curiouser. I take a photograph of the note and assure Shirley that I'll file a report on the theft. At that moment, her assistant, Paige Turner, bursts in to say there's been a theft from the staff room too. She's already called the police, so I could leave them to it, but my gut tells me to take a look.

Complete the king's journey to make your way through the library to the staff room.

4			8		11				15
	6			53			49	17	
		1			56				
95								47	
	97	91		67			59		
100	99		74			63	45		
88			75		69		37		22
		84						29	
82						33			
		78		40					25

Puzzle 128

The Skeleton Key

I retrace my steps back up to Floor 3 and turn towards the archives room. The room is completely empty, so I jump out of my skin when a series of beeps and clicks rings through the otherwise silent space. I recognise it as Morse code and listen carefully to make out the message.

Puzzle 129

.-. / --- / -... / -... / . / .-. / -.--   .. / -.
.--. / .-. / --- / --. / .-. / . / ... / ...   .- / -
...- / .. / -.-. / . / .... / .- / ... / .. .-.
.-.. / .. / -... / .-. / .- / .-. / -.--

A: .-	J: .---	S: ...	1: .----
B: -...	K: -.-	T: -	2: ..---
C: -.-.	L: .-..	U: ..-	3: ...--
D: -..	M: --	V: ...-	4: ....-
E: .	N: -.	W: .--	5: .....
F: ..-.	O: ---	X: -..-	6: -....
G: --.	P: .--.	Y: -.--	7: --...
H:	Q: --.-	Z: --..	8: ---..
I: ..	R: .-.	O: -----	9: ----.

A: ....

That certainly makes me stop in my tracks – but where on Earth is this message coming from? I follow the sound to a desk covered in newspaper articles and locate the source.

Unjumble the circled letters to find out what it is.

Puzzle 130

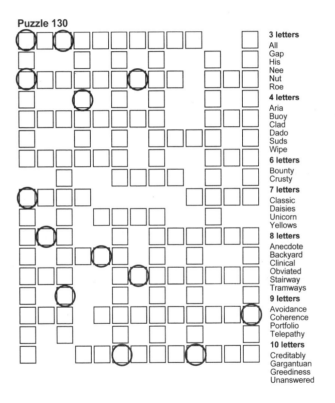

3 letters
All
Gap
His
Nee
Nut
Roe

4 letters
Aria
Buoy
Clad
Dado
Suds
Wipe

6 letters
Bounty
Crusty

7 letters
Classic
Daisies
Unicorn
Yellows

8 letters
Anecdote
Backyard
Clinical
Obviated
Stairway
Tramways

9 letters
Avoidance
Coherence
Portfolio
Telepathy

10 letters
Creditably
Gargantuan
Greediness
Unanswered

A: ....

DETECTIVE MARLOWE

When I arrive at the staff room, I find six people in deep conversation. I don't want to interrupt, so I check the photos on the staff board to see if the victim, security guard Seymour Locke, is amongst them.

Is Seymour Locke one of the people in the room?

Puzzle 131

Seymour Locke

Staff member A

Staff member B

Staff member C

Staff member D

Staff member E

Staff member F

A: ....

Three of the staff members think they witnessed the thief leaving the staff room, but their recollections are slightly different. My detective instincts tell me that only one of them actually saw the thief.

If only one of them is telling the truth, which one is it?

I didn't see their face, but their hands were full and they were moving around very shiftily.

Ravi

They seemed to know exactly where they were going. They weren't carrying anything, but they wore a backpack.

Erica

I saw it clear as day. They were carrying a duffel bag in one hand and a phone in the other.

Peter

Puzzle 132

A: ....

The Skeleton Key

A police scanner! I can't believe my luck! This will definitely help me keep one step ahead of the police. I stuff it into my backpack with the rest of my swag and notice another message on the burner phone screen.

I'm a three-digit number. My second digit is four times as big as my third. My first digit is three less than my second. I contain twice as many even numbers as odd.

Puzzle 133

A: ....

Okay, so I know I'm looking for something with a number code in this room, but as I look around, I spot lots of areas labelled with numbers. I'm going to need to narrow this down...

The item not listed in the wordsearch is the answer.

Puzzle 134

J	H	B	T	T	T	U	U	M	B	C	X	W	H
O	Q	C	C	A	R	T	O	C	P	A	T	Z	O
F	M	C	S	E	O	A	S	N	H	Z	J	E	C
M	U	B	D	N	L	F	Y	J	K	N	Y	A	T
Q	B	L	R	D	L	U	B	M	S	J	I	P	O
P	O	C	A	S	E	N	O	B	U	B	O	Q	B
H	X	B	W	H	Y	S	O	Y	U	C	N	S	F
C	V	B	E	E	A	W	K	G	P	G	A	N	M
V	I	G	R	L	R	A	C	K	A	D	Y	K	V
P	O	K	Z	F	Z	Y	A	P	H	J	P	E	X
F	Y	P	J	W	I	H	S	S	H	Z	H	A	H
O	S	I	V	A	U	V	E	S	R	C	Q	R	W
B	B	H	Y	G	R	W	P	G	X	S	X	E	V
Q	R	N	P	G	J	S	L	G	H	M	I	U	I

Bookcase	Cart	Drawer	Tray
Box	Case	Holder	Trolley
Cabinet	Desk	Rack	

A: ....

DETECTIVE MARLOWE

I make a note to get Erica in front of a sketch artist, but at least we know we're looking for someone with a backpack. Next, I speak to Seymour Locke, who confirms his bag was taken from his locker. I ask him what it looks like, and the only detail he can think of is the colour.

Unjumble the circled letters to find the answer.

Puzzle 135

	C			S		M		C			
S		R	I		P		E		O	U	S
	A		C		E		○			R	
S	T	E	T		C	I	T	○	D	E	L	S
		U			I			E			
S		A	R	I	F	Y		U	S	I	N	G
	R		○		Y		○		C		
	O	U	S			R	E		E	R	S	E
				A		D		N			
I	N	N	U	E	N	D	O		S	T	O	W
	I		E			○		I		O	
○	N	O	L	L	S		○	R	O	N		E
	G		Y		E		T		N		

A B C D E F G H I J K L M N O P Q R S T U V W X Y Z

A: ....

I ask Seymour if he can remember what was in the bag. He lists a number of items, but there are three that I take particular note of.

Identify the missing letter in each nine-letter word, then unjumble them to find the first noteworthy item.

Puzzle 136

F_ _TN_TES ....

CO_ _IDO_ ....

N_RT_RING ....

_ORE_RONT ....

I_ _OCE_CE ....

_N_T_ATOR ....

CO_ _IT_ENT ....

A: ....

The Skeleton Key

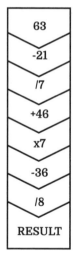

I pull open the cabinet and find dozens of document tubes. Each tube is meticulously labelled, so it shouldn't be too difficult for me to find the one I'm looking for.

Complete the brain chain to find the number code for the correct tube.

| 63 |
| -21 |
| /7 |
| +46 |
| x7 |
| -36 |
| /8 |
| RESULT |

Puzzle 137

A: ....

Success! I open the tube and remove the rolled up contents, but then I pause. Based on the Morse code message, it won't be long until the police are on my tail, but I'm sorely tempted to leave another taunting note inside the now empty tube. I need to make a quick decision, so I let Queenie Royale's lucky dice choose for me once more.

Puzzle 138

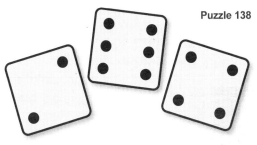

Multiply the numbers on the dice to decide what message to do:

- If it's a multiple of 2, 3, and 16: leave a message as TSK
- If it's a square number: leave a message as the Moonlight Mob
- If it's a multiple of 4 and 9: don't leave a message at all
- If it's a multiple of 14: leave a message with no name

A: ....

DETECTIVE MARLOWE

There were two more items in Seymour Locke's bag that I make a special note of.

To find the last two items, use each letter in the outer circle twice, and use the letter in the middle only once.

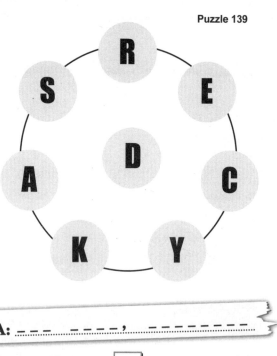

A: _ _ _   _ _ _ _ _,   _ _ _ _ _ _ _ _

I note down these items underneath the words 'Library uniform', but Seymour interrupts me. "Sorry, Detective, I should have said – the uniform in my bag wasn't for the library. I work security for a few different businesses in Vicehaven. Give me a moment to remember them all…"

The word that doesn't appear in the wordsearch is the only business Seymour doesn't work for.

Puzzle 140

B	A	A	K	W	H	M	N	F	U	K	U	Y	X
T	F	D	H	O	U	M	A	L	L	D	O	G	L
C	K	P	L	I	U	H	P	I	P	P	N	A	G
I	X	H	D	E	Y	X	L	B	R	Y	L	L	C
K	K	A	S	F	N	M	L	R	I	P	T	L	T
P	T	U	L	C	J	M	D	A	S	I	O	E	I
S	M	O	Z	A	Q	K	Y	R	O	P	F	R	S
Y	C	H	O	S	T	E	L	Y	N	S	F	Y	T
N	C	H	W	I	R	Y	W	U	E	W	I	L	T
E	G	O	O	N	X	D	S	N	A	D	C	D	U
E	O	Y	J	O	X	U	O	M	N	S	E	L	M
Z	J	P	B	U	L	S	R	E	Q	R	P	E	I
K	T	H	G	C	R	U	P	T	Y	H	S	P	Y
Z	Q	J	Y	B	S	T	O	N	O	Q	S	H	M

Airport	Gallery	Mall	School
Bank	Hostel	Museum	Stadium
Casino	Library	Prison	

A: ....

The Skeleton Key

I leave my message for the police, then send another message to the Moonlight Mob to let them know I've got everything they've asked for. I hold my breath as their coded reply comes through.

What does it say?

Puzzle 141

A: ....

I couldn't agree more. I poke my head out of the archives room and can see a large number of security guards checking people's backpacks. How am I going to get out of here without running into trouble?

Complete the pathfinder to find a route through the library that avoids the security guards.

Puzzle 142

S	I	R	A	L	C	R	I	A	F
S	I	X	O	T	O	B	Y	D	Y
A	U	O	D	E	M	Y	S	I	T
T	Q	N	S	L	I	B	K	C	I
H	E	S	E	O	N	T	H	A	N
I	G	S	Y	L	V	O	E	V	D
N	R	M	A	U	A	B	R	O	A
G	E	S	N	Y	R	E	M	A	D
O	O	C	Z	O	H	E	I	A	A
P	H	E	R	G	T	T	R	L	M

<u>Famous Books</u>

Clarissa, Don Quixote, Herzog, Madame Bovary, Moby-Dick, On The Road, Scoop, Sybil, The Ginger Man, The Trial, Ulysses, Vanity Fair

DETECTIVE MARLOWE

Seymour Locke certainly is busy. He tells me that the keycards and uniform in his bag are for his shift tonight. Finally, we're getting somewhere…

Unjumble the letters and add some vowels to find out where Seymour is supposed to be working tonight.

Puzzle 143

A: _ _ _ _ _ _ _

I'd better make some calls and let them know they've got a possible security breach. Before I leave, I just need one final detail from Seymour. Since his car keys were in his bag, I should get his number plate.

Complete the letter-doku to find the missing letters in the number plate. The correct order runs from left to right.

Puzzle 144

	A	D	C	H			B
	I	C		A	F	○	G
A	C	B		○	D		
		○					○
		G			H	C	D
	○						
	B		H	I		A	E
E			A	D	C	G	

A: _ _ 6 4 _ _ _

The Skeleton Key

Safely out on the street, I breathe a sigh of relief. That is, until I see a police car pull up. Head bowed, I scurry over to the staff parking spaces and try to identify the car of the person whose bag I have stolen as quickly as I can. I have no idea what make it is, but I should be able to figure out which lock fits the key.

Which one is it?

Puzzle 145

Seymour Locke's car lock

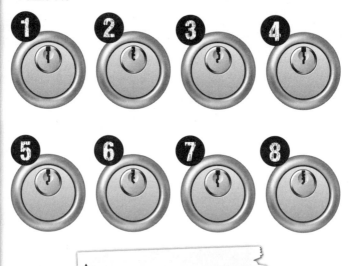

A: ....

I scramble inside the car – I'm about to be home free!
Suddenly, I remember how I nearly got caught out with
Alexis Throttle's car – I won't make that mistake again.
I bring up the car's sat nav system to disable the tracking
function, and it requests an access code. I smile to myself
– I can crack these things in my sleep...

Puzzle 146

One number is correct
but in the wrong place.

Two numbers are correct
but in the wrong place.

None of the numbers
are correct.

Two numbers are correct but
only one is in the right place.

One number is correct
and in the right place.

DETECTIVE MARLOWE

I head back to the archives room to pick up where I left off. As soon as I walk in, I notice my radio is missing and one of the cabinets is open. Unjumble the letters to find out what is usually kept in there.

3 letters
Cep
Eat

4 letters
Trap
Yell

5 letters
Angle
Passe
Segue
Worry

6 letters
Braise
Career
Rarefy
Rooted
Themes
Uplift

7 letters
Cleared
Harmful
Inherit
Intrude
Isobars
Leisure
Pierced
Rampart

8 letters
Achieved
Bedrooms
Dreadful
Infamous
Softball
Stoicism

9 letters
Assembles
Petulance

Puzzle 147

A: ....

I pull open the cabinet to check inside. None of the document tubes seem to be missing, but it looks like one has been taken out and put back in the wrong place.

I know the tubes are stored alphabetically in each row from left to right starting at the bottom. Which tubes aren't in the right place?

A: ....

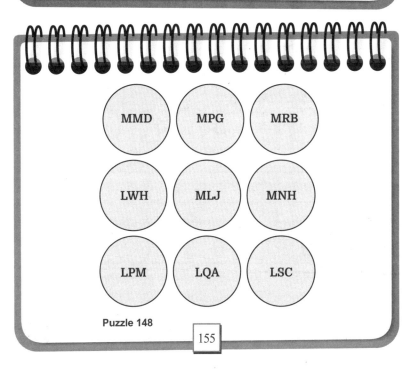

MMD	MPG	MRB
LWH	MLJ	MNH
LPM	LQA	LSC

Puzzle 148

155

The Skeleton Key

I make it home safe and am certainly glad to see my front door – what a day! But as soon as I step inside, I realise that the day isn't over yet. Someone has pushed a slip of paper under my door. I have a feeling this is another coded message from the Moonlight Mob.

Complete the sudoku to find the missing numbers. The correct order runs from left to right.

Puzzle 149

◯		6	4	9			7	2
	◯	7	◯	6	1			9
								5
	4		◯					6
	◯	2		8	◯	4		◯
7							8	
2					◯			
3		1	5		4			
4	5			6	3	2	◯	

A: ...... _ _ _ - _ _ _ - _ _ _ ......

156

It looks like a landline number, so I take out my burner phone to call it, but there's a message waiting that seems to suggest that the Moonlight Mob has other ideas.

Unjumble the circled letters to find the latest message from the Moonlight Mob.

Puzzle 150

15	14	8	26	17	15		10		21		2	
26		2			2	10	15	14	14	16	10	2
9	13	9			3		19		15		9	
17		24	4	9	9	5	9		22	15	20	2
20		8			4		14		3		9	
2	16	14	15	4		1	9	9	4	7	17	11
			17		20		3		15			
20	4	9	2	2	9	20		9	22	16	25	12
	23		10		2		18			18		15
23	12	22	9		2	6	8	7	4	3		21
	26		4		9		2			15	2	23
4	9	23	9	15	4	2	9			7		3
	20		4		3		2	15	7	17	3	2

A B C D E F G H I J K L M N O P Q R S T U V W X Y Z

1	2	3	4	5	6	7	8	9	10	11	12	13
							U					K

14	15	16	17	18	19	20	21	22	23	24	25	26
												M

A: ....

157

DETECTIVE MARLOWE

I take the lid off the MMD tube and see the contents are still there, but when I check inside MNH, the blueprints are nowhere to be found. I check the tube's label to see what the blueprints are for, but the library printer seems to have cut off the bottom of the text.

What does the label say?

Puzzle 151

VISEHAVEN

CITY MUSEUM

A: ....

158

Just as I'm about to put the lid back on the MNH tube, I notice that there is in fact something inside. I fish out the piece of paper and unroll it. Much to my surprise, it's a hand-drawn maze, and there seems to be a message concealed inside...

Follow the correct route out of the maze to discover the message.

A: ....

The Skeleton Key

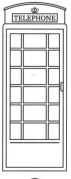

The Moonlight Mob must be worried about the security of the burner phone – which would definitely explain all the cryptic messages. I head outside my building where there's a row of payphones. Which one should I pick?

A   **B**   **C**   **D**

One of the 'Out of Order' signs is wrong.
Three of the payphones are working.
The payphones on each end are occupied.

Which is the only payphone I can use?

A: ....

I step inside the phone box, feed some change into the coin slot and dial, but nothing happens. Then, I remember you need to enter a three-digit code before making a call. It's been so long since I used a payphone, I've completely forgotten what it is, but I'm sure I can work it out.

Based on the numbers that are most worn away and the clues below, work out the 3-digit code.

Puzzle 154

The second number is half of the first.
The sum of the first and third is a multiple of the second.

A: ....

DETECTIVE MARLOWE

It feels like the ground falls out beneath me as all the pieces click into place. I hadn't for a moment connected The Skeleton Key to these thefts at the library, after all, it's nothing at all like their usual targets. Heart racing, I sit down at my desk and gather my thoughts.

Which of the following statements is the most accurate conclusion based on the evidence?

Puzzle 155

A The Skeleton Key stole a car in order to commit a crime for the Moonlight Mob.

B The Skeleton Key is going to try and steal something else from the library tomorrow.

C The Skeleton Key is going to attempt to break in to the museum tonight.

D The Skeleton Key plans to impress the Moonlight Mob with another audacious crime in the next few days.

A: ....

....

The only thing I can't work out is how the book fits into all this. Perhaps it's just worth a lot of money and The Skeleton Key couldn't resist pocketing it? I decide to look up the ISBN online to see if I can find any information. There's one result – a short news story from last month.

How much is the book's valued worth?

Vicehaven Herald

SOLD! TO VICEHAVEN LIBRARY

Ron Waffle

Vicehaven Treasure House today recorded the sale of a one-of-a-kind illustrated text (9784331702649) by discredited archaeologist Niles Carter for a shocking 50 per cent over its valued worth.

The text is a mixture of diary entries and hand-drawn illustrations depicting Carter's life-long research into – and subsequent supposed discovery of – a fabled giant hollow emerald entombed with Queen Khamunet of the Fifth Dynasty. Despite being roundly ridiculed and disparaged by the archaeology community, Carter refused to prove his findings by exhibiting the supposed treasure for fear of it being stolen, and is said to have lived out the rest of his life in a paranoid state of solitude on a remote island in Norway until his death last year.

The book was sold to Vicehaven Library for the princely (or, should I say, Pharaoh-y) sum of £24,000, much to the surprise of Chief Auctioneer, Holden Gavel. "Carter was a loon," stated Gavel. "Some people will buy any old tat."

Puzzle 156

A: ....

The Skeleton Key

I dial the number and almost immediately someone picks up on the other end. Am I about to hear the voice of Facade for the first time?

A deep voice recites the following message.

"Lovely and round,
I'm shimmery white,
grown in the darkness,
a jeweller's delight.
What am I?"

Well, this isn't what I was expecting at all, but I suppose it's only natural that Facade wants to test me some more. I think carefully, then answer...

A: ....

After a few painstaking seconds of silence, the voice speaks again.

"We've been watching you for some time, and we think you're the perfect candidate to take the lead on something we've got planned for tonight. To find out everything you need to know, bring all the trophies you took from my rivals to the location above at 7pm sharp. Don't be late."

The line goes dead, and I glance up. The roof of the phone box is covered in colourful stickers and flyers, but then I see that one notice seems to have been very deliberately marked up using a trick I know all too well.

Puzzle 158

A Bit of All ●hite Remov●ls
Have you go● old whit● goods hanging a●ound ga●her●n● dust?
Let A Bit of All W●ite Removals ●ake them off your hands! ●e'll
come ●nd col●ect a●l ●our unwanted appliances free of charge.
It●s A Bit of All White with u●!

A: ....

165

DETECTIVE MARLOWE

It's a lot for a book, but still seems like small change compared to the usual targets of these criminal masterminds. Nevermind, I need to focus on the more immediate issue of the museum's security. I look up the number for the head of security, Maxine Shield. Solve the brain chain to complete the phone number.

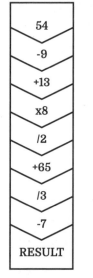

54
-9
+13
x8
/2
+65
/3
-7
RESULT

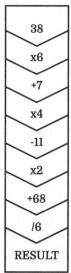

38
x6
+7
x4
-11
x2
+68
/6
RESULT

Puzzle 159

A: _ 8 _ 1 - _ 6 _ - 4 _ 7

166

I dial the number, and it's not long before Maxine picks up.

MS: Shield.

RM: Good evening, this is Detective Marlowe of the VPD.

MS: If you're calling about Locke, we already know.

RM: Actually, I have reason to believe the incident with Mr Locke may be part of a wider security breach, in fact, I—

MS: Let me stop you there, Detective. As I told your colleagues, we are well covered. In fact, tonight we have double the security staff on call.

RM: May I ask why that is?

MS: Well, between you and me, we're moving an incredibly valuable artefact into the museum this evening. Priceless, you might say.

RM: Is that so?

MS: Yes. Apparently no one thought it even existed until recently. All very hush hush. Gonna be a big launch. Don't even really know exactly what it is—

RM: Is it being moved into the Ancient Egypt exhibit, by any chance?

MS: That's... confidential. Anyway, I'm very busy, as you can imagine. Good day.

Puzzle 160

Suddenly, it all makes sense, and I know exactly what's being moved into Vicehaven City Museum tonight. What is it?

A: ....

167

The Skeleton Key

I know that Watertight Wally's is a storage facility of questionable repute on my side of town, so it won't take me long to get there. First, I need to gather up everything Facade asked for. What do I need to bring?

Tick 'true' or 'false' next to each item.

	T	F
Painting	......	......
Jewellery	......	......
Book	......	......
Cash	......	......
Diamond	......	......
Passport	......	......
Car	......	......
Deck of cards	......	......
Laptop	......	......
Dice	......	......

Together with my trophies, I roll into Watertight Wally's storage facility. There are hundreds of storage units here, which one am I supposed to go to?

Complete the king's journey and add up the circled numbers to find the correct storage unit.

Puzzle 162

	93				20	22			
	99	◯	96			23			31
	100	98			17		26	34	33
88			9	8	14			36	
	86		1	3		◯			
	84		4				42	◯	38
83					49	48		46	
80	81		56		51				
78				72			68	66	65
		74			60				

A: ....

DETECTIVE MARLOWE

I get a rush of adrenaline as the realisation hits me – for the first time since The Skeleton Key hit Queenie Royale's, I have the upper hand. I know exactly what they're going to try and steal, where and when. I take out my phone to call the head of Organised Crime, but realise I can't.

Unjumble the letters to find out why.

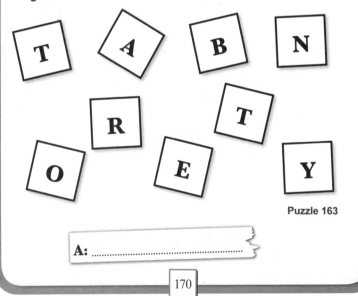

T A B N

R T

O E Y

Puzzle 163

A: ....

I need to get back to the VPD fast.
I spot a line of buses across the road.
They all go via the VPD, but which one
will get me there quickest?

Route: 14 miles
Average speed: 35 mph

Route: 12 miles
Average speed: 40 mph

Route: 11 miles
Average speed: 33 mph

Route: 15 miles
Average speed: 30 mph

Puzzle 164

A: ....

171

The Skeleton Key

I pull up outside Unit 154 and note that the roll-up door is secured with an electronic lock. To open the door, I just need to work out the six-letter code word.

Identify the missing letter in each nine-letter word, then unjumble them to find the code word.

_O_E_TITY   ....

_N_S_ALLY   ....

H_POCRIS_   ....

_U__LEGUM   ....

F__LPR__F   ....

A__EN_ION   ....

Puzzle 165

A: ....

With the lock deactivated, I pull up the door and step inside the storage unit. The only thing in there is a table with a briefcase on it. No prizes for guessing that my next instructions from the Moonlight Mob must be waiting for me inside, as soon as I can crack the lock...

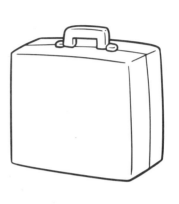

0 6 1 2 2 4 ? ? ? ?

Puzzle 166

A: ....

DETECTIVE MARLOWE

A short bus journey later, I hurry into the VPD. Of course, Inspector Conway is nowhere to be found, and everything is rather quiet. I rush over to my desk and search the directory for the extension number for the head of Organised Crime. She seems to have quite the popular name – I'll need to narrow this down...

Bush, Alfred	5602
Bush, Anne	2145
Bush, Anne	3861
Bush, Anne	5724
Bush, Anne	4387
Bush, Amber	8057

Puzzle 167

In the correct extension number:

The third digit is double the first.
The sum of all digits is a multiple of the fourth.
The sum of the first and second digits is a multiple of the third.

A: ....

I call the extension and am met with Anne Bush's answering machine. I guess I'm going to have to catch The Skeleton Key all by myself. I leave a hurried message, then rush down to the supply room to gather what I need. As I pick up my equipment, it dawns on me that there's something else I can use to my advantage. What is it?

Correct and in the right position.

Correct but not in the right position.

Not in the word.

Puzzle 168

P	O	U	C	H
D	U	S	T	Y
B	L	A	Z	E
S	P	R	I	G

| | | | | |

175

The Skeleton Key

The briefcase clicks open to reveal a single piece of paper with the following message:

The Skeleton Key,

At 20:00 tonight, the priceless Emerald Eye of Horus will be delivered under the highest security to Vicehaven City Museum. By 20:30, it should be in place and unguarded. At 21:00, the first shift of security will arrive. After that, it will be under 24/7 armed guard.

You are to steal the emerald, then drive to Smuggler's Bay, where a boat will be waiting to bring you and the emerald to me. The captain will wait until 21:30. If you – and the emerald – are not there by then, he will leave. Give the captain the code word to confirm your identity.

Everything you need to know about the emerald is in the Carter book. Memorise every detail. We don't know exactly what measures will be in place, but it will have the utmost protection.

Leave the trophies and your burner phone in this unit.

Don't let us down.

My heart is going a million miles an hour. I can't believe the Moonlight Mob are trusting me with such a huge job! Now I'm more determined than ever to impress them. I read the contents of the note again, then look at my watch. It says 6:29pm – although of course, it's still running 18 minutes slow. How long do I have to get to the museum, steal the emerald and get to Smuggler's Bay?

Puzzle 169

A: ....

Yikes. I'd better get a move on. But there's one thing in the note that confuses me – what is the code word I need to give to the captain? I turn the note over to find the answer on the back.

Puzzle 170

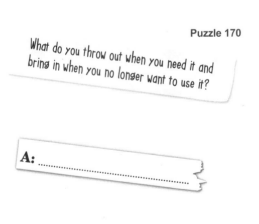

What do you throw out when you need it and bring in when you no longer want to use it?

A: ....

DETECTIVE MARLOWE

Of course! The Skeleton Key couldn't resist stealing my radio scanner, and it may well be their downfall. I know what frequency my scanner was on – there must be some way I can use it to get one step ahead of the thieving lockpick. An idea is forming in my head, but I can't quite pin it down...

Rearrange the letters in this grid to complete the idea.

Puzzle 171

D	W	S	O
M	T	W	E
H	O	N	L

A: ____ ____ ____

I spread out a map of Vicehaven and study it meticulously. With a carefully crafted fake broadcast, I can force The Skeleton Key to take the longest possible route to the museum.

Unjumble the circled letters to find out how.

Puzzle 172

A B C D E F G H I J K L M N O P Q R S T U V W X Y Z

1	2	3	4	5	6	7	8	9	10	11	12	13
L												

14	15	16	17	18	19	20	21	22	23	24	25	26
	N			R								

A: ....

179

The Skeleton Key

I leave all the items I've stolen from Facade's enemies in the storage unit and drive home as fast as I can. As I walk through the door, the police scanner crackles into life and another Morse code message fills the air. What does it say?

Puzzle 173

.- / .-.. / .-.   ..- / -. / .. / - / ...
-... / .   .- / .-- / .- / .-. / .   --- / ..-.
.-. / --- / .- / -... / .-.. / .-. / --- / -.-. / .-. / ...   ..- / -.
- / .... / .   ..-. / --- / .-. / ..-. / --- / .-- / .. / -. / --.
.-.. / --- / -.-. / .- / - / .. / --- / -. / ...

A: .-	J: .---	S: ...	1: .----
B: -...	K: -.-	T: -	2: ..---
C: -.-.	L: .-..	U: ..-	3: ...--
D: -..	M: --	V: ...-	4: ....-
E: .	N: -.	W: .--	5: .....
F: ..-.	O: ---	X: -..-	6: -....
G: --.	P: .--.	Y: -.--	7: --...
H:	Q: --.-	Z: --..	8: ---..
I: ..	R: .-.	0: -----	9: ----.

A: ....

....

I scramble to write down the coordinates read out by the scanner, but by the time I've found a pen and paper, I've missed some of the coordinates.

Complete the jigsaw sudoku to fill in the missing numbers in the coordinates. The correct order runs from left to right.

Puzzle 174

2			9			8		
○			3	5		○		6
		1		○				3
	1				2			8
	4		○	3			2	
7	○		4		○		6	
1					6			○
9		○		2	7			
		5			4		○	1

A: _0.__28, 64.7065, 40.215_,
__.9683, 39.6180, 71.6___

DETECTIVE MARLOWE

I soon arrive at the museum. If I want to get to the Emerald Eye of Horus before The Skeleton Key, I need to keep out of sight. Luckily, I happen to know there's a CCTV blind spot in the museum car park. Complete the journey to work out which parking spot is in the CCTV blind spot.

								39			
	21	31									42
16			35		94			89			
		25	29	93		98	96				
13					100			85			
10								83	78	47	
				3	74	80					
65		5	1					◯			
	67										
		61	69	59	58			53			

Puzzle 175

A: ....

182

I step out of my car, ducking into the shadows whenever the floodlights scan overhead, and head around the side of the museum building. I know I can't approach from the front, but I think I can keep out of sight if I sneak through another entrance.

Unjumble the letters to find out what it is.

Puzzle 176

G	A	T	E	A	U							
A		E				L	T	◯	◯		L	E
D	◯			B		A		S		A		
G		N	A	R	R	O				A		Z
E		I		A		I		O		E		
T	E	S	T		U	N	W	I	N	D	S	
		E		U		G		N				
	A		O	N	S		◯	T	E	R	N	
	O		◯		G			L		E		
T	O	F	U	U	N	I	Q	U	E		S	
	F			I		◯		V	A	T		
P			E	M	E	N	T		E			
	◯		S		T		S	I	◯	N	E	D

A B C D E F G H I J K L M N O P Q R S T U V W X Y Z

A: ....

The Skeleton Key

This scanner is already worth its weight in gold!
I plot the coordinates of the roadblocks onto a map and think
carefully about my route. What's the only route I can take
through Vicehaven that avoids all the police roadblocks?

FINISH

START

Puzzle 177

It's definitely the long way around, but I don't see what other choice I have. First thing's first, I need to read this Niles Carter book cover to cover and study the museum blueprints I stole from the library, all while keeping an eye on the time. I'm going to need to set a timer...

Based on the following statements, how many minutes do I have until I need to leave?

The only route to the museum that avoids the roadblocks is 24 miles long and the speed limit is 40 mph.

The church bells outside the apartment have just rung seven times.

I need to arrive at exactly 20:30, and I only have a 30-minute window to steal the emerald.

A: ....

DETECTIVE MARLOWE

I arrive at the gift shop door to find it locked and in darkness – as I expected. There's a combination lock on the outer door, but luckily, I've picked up a few skills from The Skeleton Key over the past few days...

What numbers should I turn the four question marks to?

6	3	2	5	9	7	1
4	?	8	?	?	3	?

Puzzle 179

A: ....

The lock clunks open and I slip into the pitch-black gift shop. A red light next to the door starts blinking – I know what that means. I've got 30 seconds to enter the code word before the alarm tells everyone in the museum where I am. Just as I start to panic, I notice a sticky note next to the alarm – the gift shop manager clearly has trouble remembering the alarm in the mornings and has left a clue to remind himself how to turn it off.

What's the code word?

I begin with T,
I end with T,
I only have T inside.

Puzzle 180

A: ....

187

The Skeleton Key

Aaand... I've finished the book! And with a few minutes to spare too. A sudden thought hits me – the police and museum security might be looking out for the security guard's car I stole. I wonder if I could make a few alterations to the number plate (AC64HDI) to fool them?

Add one short line to every character to turn each letter into a different letter and each number into a different number.

Puzzle 181

A: ....

That should do it! Suited up in the security guard's uniform, I get into his car and drive straight up to the museum entrance bang on 8:30pm. In this disguise, why not go through the front door? But then I see that the guards are checking the ID keycards at the door, and I have a problem.

Unjumble the letters to find out what it is.

Puzzle 182

3 letters
Era
Lee

4 letters
Chat
Spat
Ulna
Zeal

5 letters
Arose
Skies

6 letters
Cannon
Fights
Impala
Lading
Mosaic
Salami
Seller
Supine
Swerve
Unload

7 letters
Chinwag
Islands
Psychic
Scraggy

8 letters
Interned
Trapezia

9 letters
Entertain
Estimator
Fledgling
Municipal

10 letters
Groundwork
Separation

A: ....

I wind through the gift shop and push open the door into the Vikings exhibit. There are two possible routes through the Vikings exhibit that take you to two different ends of the museum. I know the Ancient Egypt wing is next to the Mesozoic Might gallery. I spot a sign, but of course it's all in Viking runes.

Which direction leads to Mesozoic Might?

Puzzle 183

ᛚ ᚼ ↑ →

← ᛦ ᚾ ᚱ

ᚼ	↑	ᛌ	ᚾ	ᚱ	ᛦ
Gifts	Warriors	Sunlight	Water	Giants	Security

A: ....

190

I make my way through the Vikings exhibit, being careful not to touch any of the exhibits in case I set off an alarm.

Complete the wordsearch to travel through the Vikings exhibit without touching anything.

Puzzle 184

U	A	R	J	L	E	H	A	L	D	E	N	Q	X	Y
R	S	B	G	A	D	R	A	I	B	A	E	T	B	N
V	T	U	V	R	L	R	K	T	R	G	X	O	L	Y
T	P	U	U	V	O	B	R	V	E	R	L	C	O	A
L	R	M	F	I	M	B	I	R	N	I	N	I	O	T
P	E	A	I	K	H	K	S	S	E	M	A	I	U	I
I	C	N	R	A	A	U	T	P	T	S	M	U	K	A
L	F	D	M	O	N	A	I	O	R	T	S	Z	U	R
D	Y	A	S	D	V	I	A	R	O	A	O	Y	B	F
A	R	L	R	A	P	N	N	S	H	D	S	E	S	T
M	O	A	N	S	U	P	S	G	I	S	R	R	O	U
I	K	G	M	M	U	L	A	R	R	G	B	V	O	U
N	E	L	X	M	E	N	N	U	E	O	F	Q	E	L
R	L	Z	M	I	E	H	D	N	O	R	T	O	A	M
E	M	O	S	S	E	N	D	N	A	S	B	P	R	H

BERGEN	HORTEN	NARVIK
DRAMMEN	KRISTIANSAND	OSLO
EGERSUND	LARVIK	PORSGRUNN
FARSUND	MANDAL	SANDNES
GRIMSTAD	MOLDE	SARPSBORG
HALDEN	MOSS	STAVANGER
HAMAR	NAMSOS	TRONDHEIM

191

The Skeleton Key

Yep – the security guard's keycards have his photograph on them, and I look nothing like him. I back away from the entrance and scan the museum blueprints I stole from the library. There are five entrances into the museum – all named after classical scholars – and I can see straight away that one offers the best chance of concealment.

To find out which entrance it is, use each letter in the outer circle multiple times, and use the letter in the middle only once.

Puzzle 185

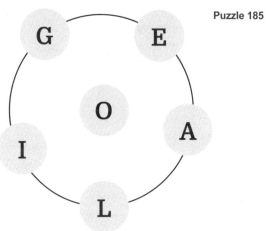

A: _ _ _ _ _ _ _ _ _ _ _ _ _ _

Yes, the more I study the blueprints the more I think this is the best way into the museum. To get to this entrance, I need to get through another part of the museum first.

Unjumble the letters and insert them amongst the vowels below to find out what it is.

T

C

B

L

N

R

D

G

N

S

Puzzle 186

A: _ O _ A _ I _ A _   _ A _ _ E _ _

DETECTIVE MARLOWE

I arrive in the Mesozoic Might gallery – my favourite part of the museum. The gallery splits off into three corridors: Jurassic, Cretaceous and Triassic. I know that the oldest fossils are down the corridor that leads to the Ancient Egypt wing. I squint at the large sign hanging high up above the giant, reconstructed skeletons, but in the darkness, I can barely make it out.

First, complete the sums to work out what number each shape represents.

Puzzle 187

● - ■ = ◆

⬡ + ◆ = 10

7 - ▲ = ●

▲ x ⬡ = 12

◖ x ■ = 0

▲ = ...

● = ...

■ = ...

◆ = ...

⬡ = ...

◖ = ...

194

Now, replace the shapes with numbers in the sign to work out which corridor to go down to reach the Ancient Egypt exhibit.

A: ....

JURASSIC   ▲ ◗ ■ - ■ ◆ ●
           .... - ....

TRIASSIC   ▲ ● ▲ - ▲ ◗ ■
           .... - ....

CRETACEOUS ■ ◆ ● - ⬡ ◆
           .... - ....

The Skeleton Key

I make my way around to the access road that backs onto the museum gardens and park up. I've lost a bit of time, so I break into a run through the museum's sprawling gardens. When I turn the corner into the topiary garden, I realise I've definitely gone the wrong way. I seem to remember that there's one odd elephant in the collection, and its trunk is pointing back at the museum, but which one is it?

Puzzle 189

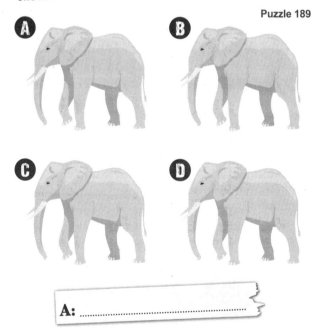

A: ....

Phew, that was lucky, I was going in entirely the wrong direction! I reorient myself and soon come across an enormous hedge maze. I can't see any way around it, so I'll have to go through it.

Find the correct route through the hedge maze.

START

FINISH

Puzzle 190

DETECTIVE MARLOWE

Before long, I arrive in the lobby of the Ancient Egypt wing. I try to remember the exact value the entire exhibit is worth, it was in the Vicehaven Herald once. Complete the kakuro to fill in the missing numbers in the amount. The correct order runs from left to right.

Puzzle 191

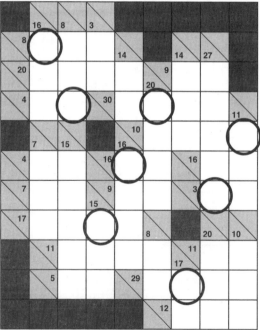

A: ....

And that was before the Emerald Eye of Horus showed up! No wonder security is so tight in this part of the museum. At the threshold to the lobby, I can see lasers criss-crossing across the tiled floor all the way to the main exhibit entrance. I think I can make it, but I'd better tread really carefully…

Complete the king's journey to find out which tiles are safe to step on to avoid the lasers.

Puzzle 192

72	71				63	59			52
				66		60			
		77		67		56	55		47
79	80	8				21			
82			5	10					44
83			1		13		23		43
				2		17		40	41
86			89						39
	100		92			30		36	35
98	99		91		28		31		

A: ....

The Skeleton Key

I finally arrive at the Galileo Galilei entrance to the museum. Catching my breath, I study the electronic lock on the outer door. It looks like a straightforward five-letter code word. This shouldn't slow me down too much.

■ Correct and in the right position.

▨ Correct but not in the right position.

□ Not in the word.

W	O	R	D	Y
F	E	A	S	T
C	H	I	M	P
S	H	A	W	L

The lock on the outer door deactivates and I push through into a decidedly more robust-looking inner door. This one has a nine-digit code that's going to take a moment to crack...

Complete the kakuro to find the number code. The correct order runs from left to right.

Puzzle 194

A: ....

DETECTIVE MARLOWE

With one final well-placed step, I stand at the entrance to the Ancient Egypt exhibit. I'm so close now! Of course, the door is locked – it looks like a keycard reader, but I know that all keycard readers have a default override code. If only I can figure out what it is…

Work out which numbers from 1 – 9 fit into each box. Each number can only be used once. The numbers in the circles reveal the correct answer, and run left to right.

Puzzle 195

		○			
	+		+		=17
X		X		+	
○	X		+		=8
-		+		-	
	-		+	○	=25

=10	=7	=18

A: ....

I step softly inside the ornate room, watchful for any other motion sensors or alarms.
There are dozens of stone archways that lead into alcoves dedicated to specific exhibits, but before I panic, I spot something that might just give away the location of the museum's latest jewel. Unjumble the circled letters to find out what it is.

Puzzle 196

5	26	16	20	6	9	11	13		1	10	20	15
6		9		1		26		17		3		1
11	1	20	7	11		7		10	5	7	13	10
		7		11		20		26		9		20
			6	8	10	23	1	6	8	10	3	7
24		20		16		1		23		13		23
23	26	3	10	20	13		20	13	12	10	23	26
21				1		6		11				2
19	1	20	17	22	19	11	3	3	14			
20		26		23		18		20		21		16
19	11	2	5	26		5		19	3	20	25	11
16		11		2		11		1		2		3
11	13		14		8	1	20	14	7	23	21	11

A B C D E F G H I J K L M N O P Q R S T U V W X Y Z

1	2	3	4	5	6	7	8	9	10	11	12	13
											J	

14	15	16	17	18	19	20	21	22	23	24	25	26
						A					V	

A: _ _ _ V _ T _ _ P E

The Skeleton Key

The door swings open and I step into the eerily silent museum. I squint around in the darkness and realise I'm not where I expected to be at all. This must be part of the museum's renovations that aren't on the blueprints. What part of the museum am I in?

Unjumble the circled letters to find out.

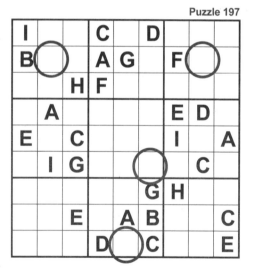

A: ....

I make my way gingerly through the room, allowing my eyes to adjust to the darkness. When I get to the other side, I creak open the door into the main building. This is more like it – I'm pretty sure I know what part of the museum I'm in now.

The area not listed in the wordsearch is the answer.

M	R	U	V	V	Y	O	D	S	H	O	P	M	T
P	R	E	H	I	S	T	O	R	I	C	K	E	A
R	E	N	A	I	S	S	A	N	C	E	L	S	A
V	I	K	I	N	G	S	W	Q	U	A	G	O	N
E	N	I	U	Z	C	H	L	Y	E	N	I	P	C
F	H	O	Y	D	C	X	B	C	I	O	F	O	I
H	J	M	X	B	M	J	E	J	N	G	T	T	E
H	T	E	Y	F	X	E	O	J	S	R	V	A	N
G	A	L	L	E	R	Y	T	H	T	A	A	M	T
F	E	Q	B	G	S	O	P	N	G	P	A	I	K
A	R	B	T	C	K	T	M	T	R	H	E	A	Z
H	R	O	G	A	Z	K	A	E	G	Y	H	J	U
I	B	P	L	A	N	E	T	A	R	I	U	M	F
V	V	D	I	N	O	S	A	U	R	S	I	X	W

Ancient	Mesopotamia	Rome
Dinosaurs	Oceanography	Shop
Gallery	Planetarium	Vikings
Gift	Prehistoric	
Greece	Renaissance	

A: ....

DETECTIVE MARLOWE

I push the velvet rope aside and face the thick stone doors. Embedded in the stone is a well-concealed keypad of Egyptian hieroglyphs. The security guards must be struggling with the hieroglyphs like I am, because I spot a crumpled bit of paper on the ground. These must be the passcodes for the past two days. If I can work them out, I might be able to guess today's.

Puzzle 199

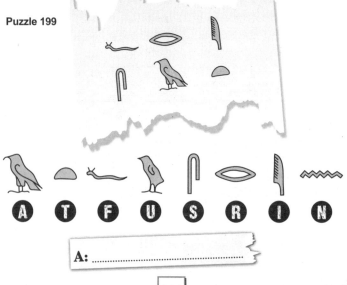

A T F U S R I N

A: ....

I enter the code, push open the stone doors and almost walk face-first into a grille door. Between the iron bars, I see a tall marble stand in the centre of the anteroom with a glass case on top. Inside, a giant emerald glows green in the moonlight. It's so beautiful I have to shake myself to get back to the task in hand – disabling this grille door.

Four letters are lit up on the door's keypad – these must be the letters I can use to make the nine-letter code word.

ENTER CODE:

....

A	B	C	D	E	F	G
H	I	J	K	L	M	N
O	P	Q	R	S	T	U
V	W	X	Y	Z	#	@

The Skeleton Key

As I stroll through the Medieval exhibit, the museum blueprints seem to come alive in my head and my confidence returns. Just then, I hear voices somewhere ahead of me. In a panic, I search around the room for something large and human-sized to hide behind.

Find the hiding place by travelling to each circle along the lines. You can only use each circle once.

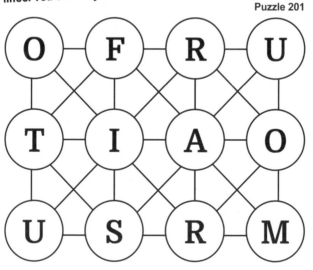

A: ....

As soon as the voices fade away, I step out from behind my hiding place. That was way too close. I hurry to the exit of the Medieval exhibit and find myself in a narrow corridor of Greek statues and busts. I would be nervous about walking down here with the lights on, but in this darkness, it's pretty terrifying...

Complete the king's journey to find a safe route through the delicate sculptures.

Puzzle 202

					71	70	63	
	93	100		80			64	
88			99		76		65	
	87		96	82			59	
		84		50			57	
45					30			55
			32			1	3	
	41	42			5			10
37	38						15	
			25	23	21	19	18	16

DETECTIVE MARLOWE

The grille doors slide up and I can feel my heart pounding in my chest as I finally lay eyes on the Emerald Eye of Horus. I bend down to examine the glass display case around it. There's a complicated-looking rotary combination lock on the case door. I take a deep breath as I try to work out the sequence.

Puzzle 203

▼

1. Anticlockwise 18
2. Clockwise 16
3. Clockwise 2
4. Anticlockwise 17
5. Clockwise 17
6. Anticlockwise 1

What word does the sequence spell?

A: ....

The case door pops open and I peer inside. This is definitely a top-of-the-range security system. Careful not to touch anything, I note that the stand's sensor is calibrated carefully to one particular parameter.

Unjumble the letters to work out what it is.

3 letters
Cue
Nun
Own
Ski
Sop
You

5 letters
Amigo
Atone
Ennui
Fudge
Fungi
Haste
Ovals
Quasi
Smash
Years

7 letters
Debased
Deepens
Garment
Scoffed
Staffed
Termini
Tickets
Trireme

8 letters
Eyeliner
Inequity
Offshoot
Recanted
Suspense
Theories

9 letters
Artlessly
Penniless

13 letters
Configuration
Dispassionate

Puzzle 204

A: ....

Not far now. I glide through the Ancient Rome exhibit as I know the Ancient Egypt lobby is on the other side. But when I reach the exit, I'm met with three doors. With a jolt of panic, I remember that the other two doors lead to a security office and the staff room – two places I need to avoid. I close my eyes and try to remember which door leads to the Ancient Egypt lobby.

Puzzle 205

XXV   XXXVI   XXIX

1. The door I need is a square number.
2. Its second digit is higher than its first.
3. The sum of its digits are a multiple of each digit.
4. Which door do I go through?

A: ....

I can't afford any more delays, and as I finally round the corner to the Ancient Egypt exhibit, I'm acutely aware that I must be running out of time. I stop short before I step into the lobby and it's just as well – a grid of motion sensor lasers covers the ground. Just as I'm contemplating whether I'm nimble enough to step through the sensors, I spot a control panel in the wall. Cracking the code to disable the sensors is a much better plan.

Unjumble the letters to find the six-letter code.

Puzzle 206

| A | B | C | D | E | F | G | H | I | J | K | L | M | N | O | P | Q | R | S | T | U | V | W | X | Y | Z |

1	2	3	4	5	6	7	8	9	10	11	12	13
		W										

14	15	16	17	18	19	20	21	22	23	24	25	26
									L	M		

A: ....

DETECTIVE MARLOWE

I know my best chance of catching The Skeleton Key is trapping them inside the grille doors, which means I need to make sure they trigger the pressure sensor. An idea hits me, and if I can pull it off, I might catch this thief once and for all. The first thing I need to do is find the three-digit code to hack into the pressure sensor.

Fill in the missing numbers to find the three-digit code in the grey hexagon.

Puzzle 207

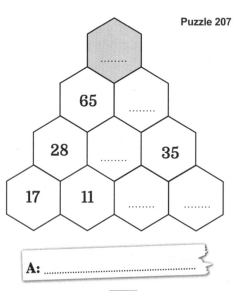

A: ....

214

I deactivate the weight sensor, and for a split second, I realise how easy it would be for me to take the emerald right there and then. I shake the thought, and dig in my pocket for something to make my plan work. I find the perfect thing, place it inside the hollow emerald and sit back. Has it worked? I realise there must be one final command to enter to set the new weight.

Unjumble the letters to work out what it is.

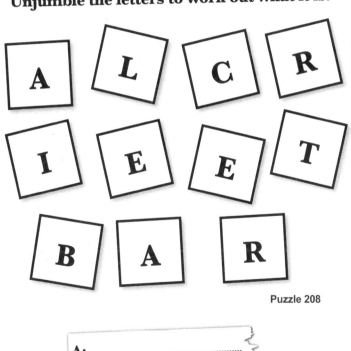

A L C R

I E E T

B A R

Puzzle 208

A: ....

The Skeleton Key

I hurry across the lobby and am somewhat relieved to find a keycard scanner at the main door. I take out the stack of keycards I stole from the security guard's bag. I know that the keycard that accesses the Ancient Egypt exhibit will have the highest level of security, so it will look different to the others.

Which keycard is for the Ancient Egypt exhibit?

Puzzle 209

A: ....

I swipe the card and the doors part with a satisfying swoosh. I must admit, I'm surprised I haven't come across any more intense security measures so far. I remind myself not to get complacent, and proceed to tiptoe carefully around the room, checking each little alcove to see if it contains my prize.

Complete the wordsearch to follow the route around the main room.

W	D	S	I	R	P	E	V	F	Y	L	I	A	S	K
B	K	A	W	V	V	G	A	Z	E	L	L	E	Y	B
J	I	H	E	F	S	U	R	O	H	F	O	E	Y	E
K	D	K	C	H	C	N	A	R	B	S	U	I	J	S
Z	A	N	A	R	D	V	L	T	U	S	I	M	I	G
F	T	C	F	D	E	R	H	A	R	P	O	O	N	J
W	N	O	H	S	R	T	A	X	K	L	C	R	Y	W
S	O	B	P	E	X	A	L	P	E	C	O	B	N	T
W	R	D	Y	D	I	C	O	E	O	G	A	O	C	G
R	E	B	R	G	L	Y	Y	B	H	E	G	J	P	I
T	H	E	Q	E	S	T	J	G	T	S	L	I	X	K
P	B	O	W	S	T	R	I	N	G	E	I	C	Y	V
N	U	G	N	I	W	P	A	L	Y	H	N	C	R	O
K	O	B	A	S	K	E	T	E	E	Z	S	E	O	Z
A	L	L	O	R	S	U	R	Y	P	A	P	W	S	H

BASKET	HARPOON	PAPYRUS ROLL
BOWSTRING	HERON	POOL
BRANCH	JACKAL	POT
EGG	KID	SAIL
EYE OF HORUS	LAPWING	SEDGE
FACE	LEOPARD HEAD	SENET BOARD
GAZELLE	ORYX	SHELTER

DETECTIVE MARLOWE

I close the display case and reset the combination lock with a new code, step outside the anteroom, then go to reactivate the grille doors. It seems that while it requires a nine-letter code to open it, you need to enter a nine-digit code to close it too.

Complete the sudoku to find the nine-digit number code. The correct order runs from left to right.

			6				9	
	9	4		7		○		5
	3	○		○				7
		6	7	4				1
	○	3	9		1	2		
9				6	2	5		
7			○		○	5		○
4			2		6	3		
	8		○		4			

A: ...... _ _ _ - _ _ _ - _ _ _ ......

What's that? I can hear a faint noise somewhere in the main room. I realise I'm trapped between the main room and the anteroom. I need to find somewhere to hide. I look around frantically, then spot the perfect – albeit slightly morbid – hiding place.

Unjumble the letters to find out what it is.

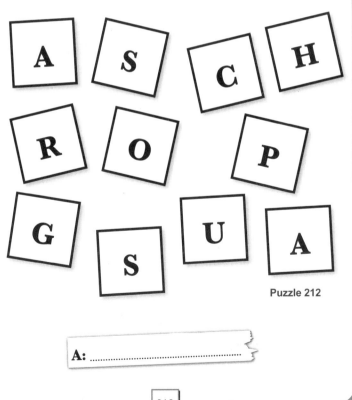

A	S		C	H
R	O			P
G		S	U	A

Puzzle 212

A: ....

The Skeleton 💀 Key

I finally come across the alcove that must contain the Emerald Eye of Horus. Someone has forgotten to set the lock on the stone door because it pushes open with no trouble. Then, I'm met with a set of grille doors. I recognise the lock system that controls the doors – I know this will be a nine-letter code word made up of the letters lit up on the keypad.

Puzzle 213

ENTER CODE:

....

A	B	C	D	E	F	G
H	I	J	K	L	M	N
O	P	Q	R	S	T	U
V	W	X	Y	Z	#	@

The grille doors slide up and I step into the moonlit room. Right in the centre, the Emerald Eye of Horus is waiting for me on a marble plinth. I walk around the glass case surrounding the emerald. It's the most sophisticated security system I've ever seen. To get inside, I first need to get through a rotary combination lock.

Puzzle 214

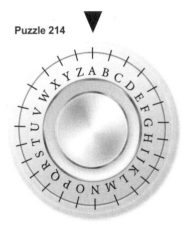

Turn the dial:

1. Anticlockwise 2
2. Anticlockwise 18
3. Clockwise 3
4. Anticlockwise 1
5. Clockwise 14
6. Clockwise 1

What word does the sequence spell?

A: ....

DETECTIVE MARLOWE

Entombed in the sarcophagus, I hear the soft whoosh of the grille doors opening. The Skeleton Key is inside the anteroom. I feel as though the sound of my pounding heartbeat must be reverberating through the whole museum. I need to calm down, and puzzles usually help me relax, so I think about the riddle from this morning's Vicehaven Herald.

Puzzle 215

Vicehaven Herald
RIDDLE OF THE DAY

What word becomes shorter when you add two letters to it?

A: ....

222

Okay, that actually helped. I can hear the The Skeleton Key moving quietly around the anteroom. I summon up another puzzle from this morning's paper to keep my mind occupied. Any minute now...

Puzzle 216

Vicehaven Herald
TRICKY TRIVIA CHALLENGE

For each row, find a word that can be added to the end of the word on the left and the beginning of the word on the right to make new words.

PUMP ___ SHIP

PROOF ____ JUST

HORSE ____ BOX

BACK ____ AGE

WET ____ SLIDE

RAIN ____ OUT

The Skeleton Key

That word has given me the jitters, but I shake them off. I've managed to get this far, what could go wrong now? I can tell straight away that the emerald is sitting on a pressure sensor, but luckily, I know from the Niles Carter book that the emerald weighs a whopping 81 grams, so if I'm very careful, I can use the weights I brought to trick the sensor.

Which pile of weights should I use?

2 grams

5 grams

10 grams

A   B   C

A: ....

Puzzle 217

224

With steady hands, I make a clean swap, but an ear-splitting piercing alarm suddenly shrieks through the room. Flashing lights blind my eyes and the grille doors slam shut. I'm trapped. I don't understand it, I got the weight right, didn't I? I look down at the emerald in my hand and notice the hinge on the side. I open it up to reveal the source of my undoing...

Unjumble the letters to find out what it is.

A: ....

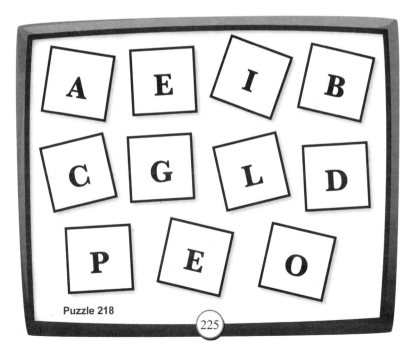

Puzzle 218

DETECTIVE MARLOWE

I can't believe it – it worked! I climb out of the sarcophagus and approach the grille bars to finally come face to face with The Skeleton Key. They look bewildered by this turn of events, and I can't help but grin when I see my police badge poking out of the hollow emerald in their hands. Just then, I hear a noise that fills me with relief. Unjumble the letters to find out what it is.

Puzzle 219

	E	C		L	E			I		N	O	R	E
O		O		A		C		I		N				
A		M		Ⓘ	I	A		R		C				
X		M		C		T	Ⓞ		P	E			E
E		A	D	Ⓒ		E	F					N
S		N				G			O	R	D	
		D		S	P	O	K	E				
G	R	O		P		R				A		
L			A		I		P	I		U	E	
O	R	G	A	N	Ⓞ			E		U		A
		L		G		A	Z	A	L	E	AⓄ	
A		O		L		L		R		L		E
L	A		E	R			P	L	A	Y	E	

A B C D E F G H I J K L M N O P Q R S T U V W X Y Z

A: _ _ _ _ _ S

A few moments later, Anne Bush bursts in with the rest of the Organised Crime squad and museum security. There's a lot of confusion and explaining to be done, but it's not long before I get the pleasure of placing The Skeleton Key under arrest. "I got your message about potentially needing special cuffs for this crook," said Anne Bush, handing me the top-of-the-line handcuffs. "You'll need to program them with a unique code that only you know."

I think back to the morning when I was first assigned to The Skeleton Key's theft from Queenie Royale's. That seems like a poignant way to bookend this cat-and-mouse chase.

Puzzle 220

7 15 20 3 8 1

What do the numbers spell out?

A: ....

The Skeleton Key

By the time 9:30pm rolls around, I'm nowhere near my getaway boat in Smuggler's Bay. Instead, I'm locked in a high-security cell at the VPD. Will Facade come for me? Or will they leave me here to rot?

There's a rattle at my door, and a tray is passed through the food slot with a measly supper and a copy of the Vicehaven Herald. "Something to keep you occupied," mutters the voice on the other side. I pick at the meagre offerings, then unfold the paper. On the front page, someone has scribbled a curious note in the margins.

Puzzle 221

What is the only number spelled alphabetically?

In
of eve
Galler
by thi
with t
and jo
Grift
The
vanisl
leavin
nity h
mand
detect
the in

A: ....

How random. Unless... could it be a page number? I flick through the newspaper until I come to a puzzle page. It wouldn't be the first time I was sent a coded message via the Vicehaven Herald, so I eagerly complete it and smile when I realise what it says.

Unjumble the circled letters to decode the message.

Puzzle 222

| A | B | C | D | E | F | G | H | I | J | K | L | M | N | O | P | Q | R | S | T | U | V | W | X | Y | Z |

1	2	3	4	5	6	7	8	9	10	11	12	13
						I						

14	15	16	17	18	19	20	21	22	23	24	25	26
				Y	T							

A: ....

DETECTIVE MARLOWE

Back at the VPD, Inspector Conway knocks on my door. "Very good work tonight," he says. "A real team effort." I bite my tongue and say, "Thank you, sir." He hands me a small box. "Now we can put this whole Moonlight Mob business to bed." He shuffles out of my office and I open the small box. What's inside?

■ Correct and in the right position.

▨ Correct but not in the right position.

☐ Not in the word.

F	L	O	U	R
D	R	A	N	K
C	H	I	M	P
B	E	I	N	G

I'm not so confident that the story with The Skeleton Key and Moonlight Mob is over yet, but that's a problem for tomorrow.

For now, there's only one more thing I need to do today. What is it?

A: ....

I weaken all people for hours each day.

I show you strange visions when I come to stay.

I take you by night, by day give you back.

None suffer to have me, but do from my lack.

What am I?

Puzzle 224

Solutions

Puzzle 1

LADY LUCK'S CASINO

Puzzle 2

8	6	9	7	4	3	1	5	2
3	5	4	1	8	2	7	9	6
2	7	1	9	6	5	3	8	4
5	3	8	2	9	1	6	4	7
1	9	7	6	5	4	8	2	3
4	2	6	3	7	8	5	1	9
6	8	5	4	2	7	9	3	1
9	4	3	8	1	6	2	7	5
7	1	2	5	3	9	4	6	8

4536

Puzzle 3

CASE NUMBER: **FD28B**

CRIME: **THEFT**

Puzzle 4

9571-427-638

Solutions

Puzzle 5

E

Puzzle 6

792

Puzzle 7

FORTUNE STREET

Puzzle 8

E

Solutions

Puzzle 9

TWENTY-EIGHT BLACK

Puzzle 10

B (THE KING OF CLUBS)

Puzzle 11

£12,825

Puzzle 12

C

Solutions

Puzzle 13

D

Puzzle 14

4923

Puzzle 15

A DIAMOND

Puzzle 16

QUEENIE ROYALE'S
LUCKY GOLDEN DICE

Solutions

Puzzle 17

THE CLEAN-UP CREW

Puzzle 18

BUSTER BUTLER

Puzzle 19

FINGERPRINTS

Puzzle 20

NO

Solutions

Puzzle 21

NO, HE'S NOT IN

Puzzle 22

SQUALID

Puzzle 23

SAFE HOUSE MOTEL

Puzzle 24

ROUTE A

Solutions

Puzzle 25

MESSAGE FOR MR BUTLER.
YOUR DRIVER WILL PICK YOU
UP TONIGHT AT QUARTER TO
ELEVEN EXACTLY.

Puzzle 26

7 MINUTES

Puzzle 27

FOOTPRINT

Puzzle 28

MESSAGE RECEIVED
BACKUP ON STANDBY

Solutions

Puzzle 29

BERLIN

Puzzle 30

NEWSPAPER

Puzzle 31

PAINTING

Puzzle 32

THE SKELETON
KEY SENDS THEIR
REGARDS

Solutions

Puzzle 33

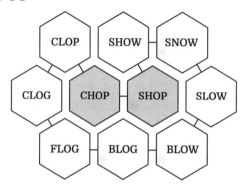

THE CHOP SHOP

Puzzle 34

50	49	48	47	37	36	30	29	27	26
51	52	92	91	46	38	35	31	28	25
53	100	98	93	90	45	39	34	32	24
54	97	99	94	89	74	44	40	33	23
55	85	96	95	88	75	73	43	41	22
56	84	86	87	81	76	72	71	42	21
7	57	83	82	80	77	70	67	65	20
6	8	58	79	78	69	68	66	64	19
2	5	9	59	60	61	62	63	18	17
1	3	4	10	11	12	13	14	15	16

Solutions

Puzzle 35

CONFIDENTIAL

Puzzle 36

SIZE 8

Puzzle 37

1043

Puzzle 38

G 3 T 4 W 4 Y

Puzzle 39

EBFACD

Solutions

Puzzle 40

MESSAGE FOR DET. MARLOWE.
BREAK-IN REPORTED AT THE CHOP
SHOP. PLEASE ATTEND.

Puzzle 41

87

Puzzle 42

SPRAY PAINT

Puzzle 43

F	I	D	E	C	B	H	G	A
G	A	B	F	I	H	E	D	C
C	H	E	D	A	G	I	B	F
A	B	C	G	H	I	F	E	D
D	E	I	A	F	C	G	H	B
H	G	F	B	D	E	C	A	I
B	F	H	C	G	A	D	I	E
E	C	G	I	B	D	A	F	H
I	D	A	H	E	F	B	C	G

DI3-5E7

Solutions

Puzzle 44

ALEXIS

Puzzle 45

THE BROKERS

Puzzle 46

Solutions

Puzzle 47

PHANTOM X2

Puzzle 48

THE SKELETON KEY TAG

Puzzle 49

DOOR 4

Puzzle 50

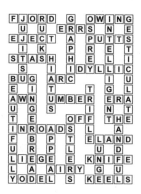

HUSH MONEY HUT

Solutions

Puzzle 51

SAT NAV

Puzzle 52

70382

Puzzle 53

HEXAGON

Puzzle 54

BOOK

Solutions

Puzzle 55

83 MINUTES
(1 HOUR 23 MINUTES)

Puzzle 56

BUILDING H

Puzzle 57

SENATOR, CHIEF, DIRECTOR,
PRESIDENT, MAYOR, GOVERNOR,
ARCHBISHOP, JUDGE,
CHANCELLOR, AMBASSADOR

Puzzle 58

SILENCE

Solutions

Puzzle 59

7	4	1	5	6	9	3	2	8
6	9	5	3	2	8	7	4	1
3	8	2	4	1	7	5	6	9
9	2	3	7	4	1	6	8	5
8	1	6	2	3	5	9	7	4
4	5	7	8	9	6	2	1	3
2	6	4	9	8	3	1	5	7
5	3	8	1	7	2	4	9	6
1	7	9	6	5	4	8	3	2

9156

Puzzle 60

32784 (EARTH)

Puzzle 61

C, E and F

Puzzle 62

FIRE ESCAPE

Solutions

Puzzle 63

DOOR 2 (THE SIGN ON
DOOR 3 IS TRUTHFUL)

Puzzle 64

HEADLIGHTS

Puzzle 65

3	6	8	1	9	2	4	7	5
5	9	1	4	7	6	3	8	2
2	4	7	3	5	8	9	1	6
6	7	2	9	8	5	1	3	4
8	5	4	7	1	3	6	2	9
1	3	9	6	2	4	7	5	8
7	1	5	8	6	9	2	4	3
4	8	6	2	3	1	5	9	7
9	2	3	5	4	7	8	6	1

40

Puzzle 66

BREAKNECK

Solutions

Puzzle 67

BEADC

Puzzle 68

£664,420

Puzzle 69

ADVERTS

Puzzle 70

WELL DONE TSK, GO TO
ROSEBUD FLORIST

Solutions

Puzzle 71

	T	F
The Skeleton Key left their fingerprints at two scenes.		✓
Queenie Royale and Alexis Throttle are connected to criminal gangs.	✓	
A diamond and cash were taken from Queenie Royale's safe.		✓
The Skeleton Key must have walked to Hush Money Hut.		✓
Alex Throttle operates out of The Chop Shop.	✓	
The Skeleton Key is connected to an unsolved kidnapping.		✓
The Clean-up Crew is implicated in a theft from Vicehaven Gallery.	✓	
The Skeleton Key has size 9 feet.		✓

Puzzle 72

3	4	6	7	46	47	48	49	50	51
2	5	8	45	60	59	58	57	53	52
1	9	44	61	87	86	82	81	56	54
10	43	62	88	99	98	85	83	80	55
11	42	63	89	100	97	96	84	79	74
12	41	64	90	93	94	95	78	75	73
13	37	40	65	91	92	77	76	72	71
14	36	38	39	66	67	68	69	70	28
15	18	35	34	33	32	31	30	29	27
16	17	19	20	21	22	23	24	25	26

37 HOURS

Puzzle 73

THEO KELSEY KENT

Puzzle 74

TRAIN STATION

250

Solutions

Puzzle 75

SAMPLE G

Puzzle 76

KIDNAPPING

Puzzle 77

START

FINISH

Solutions

Puzzle 78

FIRST CLASS TRAIN TICKET

Puzzle 79

MONEY

Puzzle 80

613145 = FACADE

Puzzle 81

U63

Solutions

Puzzle 82

BURNER PHONE

Puzzle 83

LUNA NIGHTCLUB

Puzzle 84

1. THE HIGH ROLLERS – QUEENIE ROYALE – LADY LUCK'S CASINO
2. THE CLEAN-UP CREW – BUSTER BUTLER – SAFE HOUSE MOTEL
3. THE BROKERS – HANDOUT HAL – HUSH MONEY HUT
4. THE AXEL GRINDERS – ALEXIS THROTTLE – THE CHOP SHOP
5. THE MOONLIGHT MOB – FACADE – LUNA'S NIGHTCLUB

Puzzle 85

6	1	2	5	9	3	7	4	8
3	9	8	2	4	7	1	5	6
7	4	5	8	1	6	3	2	9
5	2	4	7	6	1	8	9	3
9	8	6	3	2	5	4	7	1
1	7	3	4	8	9	5	6	2
2	6	7	1	5	8	9	3	4
4	5	1	9	3	2	6	8	7
8	3	9	6	7	4	2	1	5

1384

Solutions

Puzzle 86

LIBRARY

Puzzle 87

Sir,
I HAVE REASON TO BELIEVE THIS LATEST SPATE OF CRIMES IS THE WORK OF A NEW PLAYER WITH CONNECTIONS TO THE MOONLIGHT MOB. PERMISSION TO FORM A TOP SECRET TASK FORCE TO INVESTIGATE?

Puzzle 88

TAKE A DAY OFF AND REST

Puzzle 89

FELONY LANE

Solutions

Puzzle 90

16:03 (4:03pm)

Puzzle 91

3	6	8	7	4	1	2	5	9
9	4	7	2	5	8	3	1	6
2	5	1	9	3	6	7	8	4
5	7	3	6	1	4	8	9	2
1	9	6	3	8	2	5	4	7
8	2	4	5	9	7	6	3	1
6	8	9	4	2	3	1	7	5
4	3	2	1	7	5	9	6	8
7	1	5	8	6	9	4	2	3

156.478 MHz

Puzzle 92

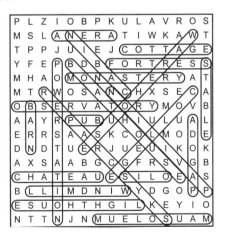

255

Solutions

Puzzle 93

BOOK (THE REST CAN ALL BE MADE INTO COMPOUND WORDS BY ADDING 'EYE')

Puzzle 94

THE DICTIONARY

Puzzle 95

WHODUNIT

Puzzle 96

FRANKENSTEIN

Puzzle 97

175

Solutions

Puzzle 98

CIPHER

Puzzle 99

4	6	3	2	9	1	5	7	8
7	9	2	5	8	4	1	3	6
8	5	1	3	6	7	9	2	4
3	7	4	6	1	2	8	9	5
9	1	8	7	4	5	2	6	3
5	2	6	9	3	8	7	4	1
2	8	9	4	5	3	6	1	7
1	3	7	8	2	6	4	5	9
6	4	5	1	7	9	3	8	2

23815

Puzzle 100

CONVICTED, CAUGHT

257

Solutions

Puzzle 101

SEVEN

Puzzle 102

NILES CARTER

Puzzle 103

THEY NEVER LEAVE
ANY EVIDENCE

Puzzle 104

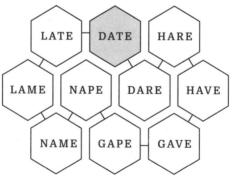

DATE

Solutions

Puzzle 105

RARE BOOKS

Puzzle 106

786329 (SUNDAY)

Puzzle 107

21/08
23/04
20/09
22/06
22/07
23/05

Puzzle 108

HUNTER'S MOON

Solutions

Puzzle 109

TNAMSB

Puzzle 110

LOST TREASURES OF
KHAMUNET'S TOMB

Puzzle 111

ANNE BUSH

Puzzle 112

TONIGHT

Solutions

Puzzle 113

QUIET	SHELVES
INDEX	BORROW
LIBRARIAN	LEARN
PUBLIC	STORIES
VOLUME	CATALOGUE
BOOKS	KNOWLEDGE

THE STAFF ROOM

Puzzle 114

FLOOR 2

Puzzle 115

DETECTIVE MARLOWE
SOMEONE HAS TAKEN SOMETHING
FROM THE RARE BOOKS ROOM
CAN YOU HELP US

Solutions

Puzzle 116

C – OF COURSE, I AM
HAPPY TO HELP

Puzzle 117

19645

Puzzle 118

LOCKERS

Puzzle 119

D

Solutions

Puzzle 120

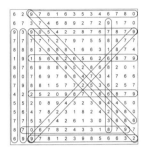

9784331702649

Puzzle 121

541

Puzzle 122

4352

Puzzle 123

5	7	8	6	3	9	1	2	4
4	9	6	1	2	5	7	8	3
1	3	2	4	8	7	5	6	9
6	4	3	8	7	1	9	5	2
2	5	7	9	6	3	4	1	8
8	1	9	2	5	4	3	7	6
9	6	4	7	1	2	8	3	5
3	2	1	5	9	8	6	4	7
7	8	5	3	4	6	2	9	1

932-158

Solutions

Puzzle 124

ANCIENT EGYPT

Puzzle 125

F	D	B	H	A	G	I	C	E
G	I	H	E	C	B	A	D	F
C	E	A	D	I	F	G	B	H
E	H	D	G	F	I	C	A	B
B	C	G	A	D	H	E	F	I
A	F	I	C	B	E	H	G	D
I	A	F	B	H	C	D	E	G
H	G	C	F	E	D	B	I	A
D	B	E	I	G	A	F	H	C

BAG

Puzzle 126

ARCHIVES

Puzzle 127

E, N AND R

Solutions

Puzzle 128

4	3	7	8	10	11	12	13	14	15
5	6	2	9	53	52	51	49	17	16
94	93	1	54	55	56	57	50	48	18
95	96	92	66	65	61	60	58	47	19
98	97	91	73	67	64	62	59	46	20
100	99	90	74	72	68	63	45	36	21
88	89	85	75	71	69	44	37	35	22
87	86	84	76	70	43	38	34	29	23
82	83	79	77	42	39	33	30	28	24
81	80	78	41	40	32	31	27	26	25

Puzzle 129

ROBBERY IN PROGRESS
AT VICEHAVEN LIBRARY

Puzzle 130

```
C R E D I T A B L Y       T
L     A   R   A     G     E
A V O I D A N C E   A L L
S     S   M   K     R     E
S T A I R W A Y     G A P
I     E   A   A R I A     A
C R U S T Y   R     N U T
      N     S U D S T   H
C L A D           B U O Y
O   N   D A D O       A
H I S       N   B O U N T Y
E   W I P E   V   N       E
R O E     C L I N I C A L
E   R     D   A   C     L
N E E   P O R T F O L I O
C   D     T   E   R     W
E     G R E E D I N E S S
```

POLICE SCANNER

265

Solutions

Puzzle 131

YES – STAFF MEMBER F

Puzzle 132

ERICA

Puzzle 133

582

Puzzle 134

CABINET

Solutions

Puzzle 135

DARK BLUE

Puzzle 136

UNIFORM

Puzzle 137

41

Puzzle 138

48 – LEAVE A MESSAGE AS TSK

Puzzle 139

CAR KEYS KEYCARDS

Solutions

Puzzle 140

BANK

Puzzle 141

TIME TO GO

Puzzle 142

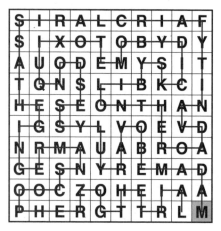

Puzzle 143

MUSEUM

Solutions

Puzzle 144

G	E	A	D	C	H	F	I	B
H	I	C	B	A	F	D	G	E
B	D	F	E	G	I	C	H	A
A	C	B	I	H	D	E	F	G
D	G	H	C	F	E	B	A	I
I	F	E	G	B	A	H	C	D
C	A	G	F	E	B	I	D	H
F	B	D	H	I	G	A	E	C
E	H	I	A	D	C	G	B	F

AC64HDI

Puzzle 145

LOCK 7

Puzzle 146

3071

Puzzle 147

BLUEPRINTS

Solutions

Puzzle 148

MMD AND MNH

Puzzle 149

1	3	6	4	9	5	8	7	2
5	2	8	7	3	6	1	4	9
9	7	4	2	1	8	3	6	5
8	4	3	1	5	9	7	2	6
6	9	2	3	8	7	4	5	1
7	1	5	6	4	2	9	8	3
2	6	9	8	7	1	5	3	4
3	8	1	5	2	4	6	9	7
4	5	7	9	6	3	2	1	8

198-137-511

Puzzle 150

PAYPHONE

Puzzle 151

VICEHAVEN CITY MUSEUM

270

Solutions

Puzzle 152

START

FINISH

YOU WILL NEVER CATCH
THE SKELETON KEY

Puzzle 153

PAYPHONE B

271

Solutions

Puzzle 154

428

Puzzle 155

C – THE SKELETON KEY IS
GOING TO ATTEMPT TO BREAK
INTO THE MUSEUM TONIGHT

Puzzle 156

£16,000

Puzzle 157

PEARL

Puzzle 158

WATERTIGHT WALLY'S

Solutions

Puzzle 159

9851-362-417

Puzzle 160

THE EMERALD EYE OF HORUS

Puzzle 161

	T	F
Painting	✓	
Jewellery		✓
Book	✓	
Cash	✓	
Diamond	✓	
Passport		✓
Car	✓	
Deck of cards		✓
Laptop		✓
Dice	✓	

Solutions

Puzzle 162

92	93	94	95	19	20	22	28	29	30
91	99	97	96	18	21	23	27	32	31
90	100	98	12	13	17	24	26	34	33
88	89	11	9	8	14	16	25	36	35
87	86	10	1	3	7	15	40	39	37
85	84	54	4	2	6	41	42	43	38
83	82	55	53	5	49	48	47	46	44
80	81	57	56	52	51	50	69	67	45
78	79	75	58	72	71	70	68	66	65
77	76	74	73	59	60	61	62	63	64

UNIT 155

Puzzle 163

NO BATTERY

Puzzle 164

BUS 363

Puzzle 165

BOUNTY

Puzzle 166

4896

Puzzle 167

3861

Solutions

Puzzle 168

RADIO

Puzzle 169

2 HOURS 43 MINUTES
(163 MINUTES)

Puzzle 170

ANCHOR

Puzzle 171

SLOW THEM DOWN

Puzzle 172

ROADBLOCKS

Solutions

Puzzle 173

ALL UNITS BE AWARE
OF ROADBLOCKS IN THE
FOLLOWING LOCATIONS

Puzzle 174

2	3	7	9	4	6	8	1	5
4	9	8	3	5	1	2	7	6
6	5	1	2	7	8	9	4	3
3	1	9	7	6	2	4	5	8
5	4	6	8	3	9	1	2	7
7	8	2	4	1	5	3	6	9
1	7	4	5	8	3	6	9	2
9	6	3	1	2	7	5	8	4
8	2	5	6	9	4	7	3	1

40.8328, 64.7065, 40.2158,
75.9683, 39.6180, 71.6232

Puzzle 175

18	19	20	32	33	37	38	39	40	41
17	21	31	34	36	91	90	88	43	42
16	22	30	35	92	94	95	89	87	44
15	23	25	29	93	99	98	96	86	45
13	14	24	26	28	100	97	85	84	46
10	12	8	7	27	81	82	83	78	47
11	9	6	4	3	74	80	79	77	48
65	66	5	1	2	73	75	76	55	49
64	67	68	60	70	71	72	56	54	50
63	62	61	69	59	58	57	53	52	51

76

Solutions

Puzzle 176

GIFT SHOP

Puzzle 177

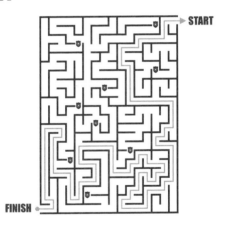

Puzzle 178

54 MINUTES

Puzzle 179

7519

Solutions

Puzzle 180

TEAPOT

Puzzle 181

BE89ABL

Puzzle 182

PHOTOGRAPH

Puzzle 183

LEFT (GIANTS)

Solutions

Puzzle 184

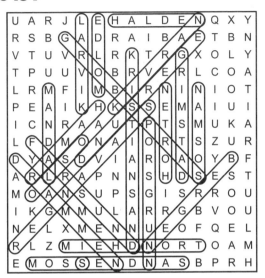

Puzzle 185

GALILEO GALILEI

Puzzle 186

BOTANICAL GARDENS

Puzzle 187

▲ = 2   ● = 5   ■ = 1

◆ = 4   ⬡ = 6   ◗ = 0

Solutions

Puzzle 188

JURASSIC: 201-145
TRIASSIC: 252-201
CRETACEOUS: 145-66

TRIASSIC

Puzzle 189

D

Puzzle 190

Solutions

Puzzle 191

£41,976,923

Puzzle 192

64,62,61,20,12,4,14,16,26,29

Puzzle 193

RELIC

Solutions

Puzzle 194

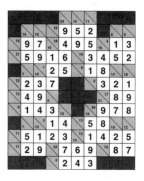

533462889

Puzzle 195

237

Puzzle 196

VELVET ROPE

Solutions

Puzzle 197

I	E	F	C	B	D	A	H	G
B	C	D	A	G	H	F	E	I
A	G	H	F	I	E	C	B	D
F	A	B	G	C	I	E	D	H
E	H	C	B	D	F	I	G	A
D	I	G	E	H	A	B	C	F
C	D	A	I	E	G	H	F	B
G	F	E	H	A	B	D	I	C
H	B	I	D	F	C	G	A	E

CAFE

Puzzle 198

BANK

Puzzle 199

SUN

Puzzle 200

SLEEPLESS

Puzzle 201

SUIT OF ARMOUR

Solutions

Puzzle 202

90	91	92	79	78	72	71	70	63	62
89	93	100	98	80	77	73	69	64	61
88	94	97	99	81	76	74	68	65	60
86	87	95	96	82	75	67	66	59	58
46	85	84	83	50	51	52	53	57	56
45	47	48	49	31	30	7	8	54	55
40	44	43	32	29	6	1	3	9	11
39	41	42	33	28	5	4	2	12	10
37	38	34	27	24	22	20	17	15	13
36	35	26	25	23	21	19	18	16	14

Puzzle 203

SCARAB

Puzzle 204

```
A T O N E   S C O F F E D
R       Y   U   F       E
T I C K E T S   F U D G E
L   O   L   P   S   I   P
E N N U I   E   H A S T E
S   F   N U N   O   P   N
S K I   E   S   O V A L S
L   G A R M E N T   S
Y O U           S O P
    R   T E R M I N I   E
S M A S H   E   N   O W N
T   T   E   C U E   N   N
A M I G O   A   Q U A S I
F   O   R   N   U   T   L
F U N G I   T R I R E M E
E       E   E   T       S
D E B A S E D   Y E A R S
```

PRESSURE

284

Solutions

Puzzle 205

XXXVI / 36

Puzzle 206

TIPTOE

Puzzle 207

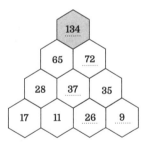

134

Puzzle 208

RECALIBRATE

Puzzle 209

B

Solutions

Puzzle 210

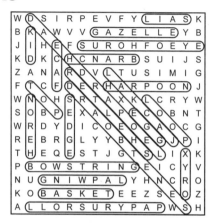

Puzzle 211

1	4	7	6	3	5	8	9	2
6	2	9	4	8	7	1	3	5
5	3	8	1	2	9	6	4	7
2	5	6	7	4	3	9	8	1
8	7	3	9	5	1	2	6	4
9	1	4	8	6	2	5	7	3
7	6	2	3	1	8	4	5	9
4	9	5	2	7	6	3	1	8
3	8	1	5	9	4	7	2	6

178-519-439

Puzzle 212

SARCOPHAGUS

Puzzle 213

ASSASSINS

286

Solutions

Puzzle 214

CURSED

Puzzle 215

SHORT

Puzzle 216

PUMP <u>KIN</u> SHIP
PROOF <u>READ</u> JUST
HORSE <u>SHOE</u> BOX
BACK <u>PACK</u> AGE
WET <u>LAND</u> SLIDE
RAIN <u>FALL</u> OUT

Puzzle 217

C

Puzzle 218

POLICE BADGE

Solutions

Puzzle 219

SIRENS

Puzzle 220

GOTCHA

Puzzle 221

FORTY

Puzzle 222

JAILBREAK

Puzzle 223

MEDAL

Puzzle 224

SLEEP

288